Dona Paula

Saúde e Paz

04.05.2012

Dona Paula

Joseph C. Dias

author**HOUSE**®

AuthorHouse™
1663 Liberty Drive
Bloomington, IN 47403
www.authorhouse.com
Phone: 1-800-839-8640

First Edition, 2008

First published by AuthorHouse   06/20/2011

ISBN: 978-1-4567-8493-5 (sc)
ISBN: 978-1-4567-8494-2 (ebk)

Printed in the United States of America

ABOUT THE AUTHOR:

Joseph Canisius Dias is an Architect, cartoonist, sculptor, musician and a writer of articles, short stories and poetry in his spare time. He has illustrated many children's feature stories which have been published in the local children's magazines. His website www.word.diaz.co.in also carries some of his work. Dona Paula is his first novel but there are many more in their editing stages. It is a historical romance set in 1667 Goa, the ex-Portuguese colony in India.

ACKNOWLEDGEMENT:

This book would not have been possible without:

My parents, Joana Fernandes e Dias
and the late Peter F.V. Dias for the gift of 'me'.
My brother Cosme,
who encouraged me to write this story.
The Goan legend, the late Dr. Manoharrai Sardessai,
who always urged me to write.
My research material provider, architect and dear friend,
Mr. Sunil Sardessai.
My trial readers, Mrs. Rangachari, Mrs. Rugmani Rao,
Ms. Jasleen Uppal, Ms.Sandra Reis D'Costa and Caroline
Sanfrancisco.
My brother Antonio, the 'Goa Expert,' who provided much
guidance during the course of this work.
My friend Sylvester Rodrigues who meticulously went over the
manuscript during the early phases.
My graphic/layout artist Stanley Pinto, who made all those
numerous revisions without complaint.
To all those who may have had a part in the realisation of this
book but whose names I have not mentioned.
My beloved wife Lorine and our wonderful sons, Leander and
Leroy, who stood by me patiently, although I encroached on 'prime
family time' during the research and writing of this book.

To my beloved maternal grandmother,
the late Ritinha Furtado e Fernandes,
who was a wonderful storyteller.

TABLE OF CONTENTS

PROLOGUE

Ask any Goan about The Legend of Dona Paula and he will tell you any one of the various myths that have been passed on to them by word of mouth from one generation to another. What may have once been an exact account is today but a figment of someone's imagination, with much scope for further embellishment.

Not disputing my grandmother's version of the story, which I have now fictionalized into this novel, I have also included in brief, a few of the myths 'whispered' to me by some senior citizens of Goa:

-Dona Paula was the daughter of a Portuguese viceroy, who fell in love with a goan fisherman. She was heartbroken when she was refused permission to marry him and committed suicide by throwing herself off a cliff in Oddavel.

-Dona Paula, the daughter of a Portuguese viceroy, was pushed off a cliff when she was found guilty of captivating the Count of Alvor with her irresistible charm.

-Dona Paula was the lady-in-waiting to the Governor General's wife. In a fit of jealousy over their suspected affair, the Governor's wife is believed to have had her stripped naked except for the necklace of pearls that was gifted to Paula by her unfaithful husband and had her rolled off the cliff, after binding her limbs.

-Gaspar Dias, a Portuguese nobleman believed to have been in love with Dona Paula, betrayed her love and married another. Paula committed suicide by jumping off a cliff at Oddavel and to this day, it is believed that her ghost is seen looking desperately for the nobleman, seeking revenge.

-The present day marmorite sculpture of a man and woman facing opposite directions, atop a cliff in Oddavel, was put up there to immortalize the love story between Dona Paula, a Portuguese lady of high birth and her lover, a local fisherman, who went out to sea and never returned home. She is believed to have spent the rest of her days atop the cliff and got changed into stone!

(In reality, these statues were commissioned by the late Mr. Knox, an US senator, who appointed a German sculptor Yrsa Von Leistner to do several works of art to be put up in selected countries).

-Dona Paula was the wife of a Portuguese aristocrat, who the villagers loved for her many acts of kindness. After her tragic death by falling off the cliff in Oddavel, the villagers paid tribute to her by naming the village after her name.

It is interesting to note however, that the village called Oddavel did exist and was renamed by the villagers after a certain Dona Paula who lived and died sometime during the 450 years of Portuguese occupation.

My version of the story is set in Goa in the year 1667, by which time the Portuguese empire in the east had grown in strength. Alphonso De Albuquerque had forcefully wrested away the famous and prized port at the mouth of the Mandovi River from Adil Shah in 1510, ending the prosperity of the Muslims and making the city the capital of their sea-borne empire in the east. The Portuguese raked in huge profits from this strategically located port on the west coast and routed most of the trade along these shores through the port of 'Gova'. Gova was renamed 'Goa' by the Portuguese and soon earned the reputation of being called *'Goa Dourada'* or *'Golden Goa'*.

Two magnificent rivers, the Zuari and the Mandovi emptied themselves into the great Arabian Sea after meandering through green landscapes. The relocation of the then famous seaport on the banks of the Zuari River to the mouth of the Mandovi, due to silting of the Zuari, gave birth to a new city which flourished in trade. The ships took back to Arabia, calico, fine muslins, rice, areca nuts and spices in exchange for the fine Arabian horses which were in demand with the kings and chieftains of the Deccan.

The Portuguese were the first European power to come to India bringing with them their religion and also their way of life; both of which had a profound impact on Goan culture. By 1543, they had added the provinces of

Tiswadi, Bardez and Salcette, called the 'Old Conquests', to their possessions. The Portuguese went about the task of converting the Hindus and Muslims with fanatical zeal but the converts continued to practice their old religious customs. Although the Portuguese made it virtually impossible for converts to practice their religion even in the privacy of their own homes, the Hindus continued to cling to their old faith in hiding. The Enraged Portuguese, employed harsher measures to curb this disobedience. Churches were erected over the very footprints of destroyed temples. Hindu lands were confiscated and granted to Christian institutions. The Hindus, though demoralized, stubbornly held on to their convictions. New shrines were erected in the neighboring heavily forested and hilly regions of Ponda and Bicholim for the deities and idols smuggled from destroyed temples. In 1560, the cruel and much feared Inquisition was introduced by the Portuguese government. It was more severe than the Inquisition in Spain and Portugal and lasted for about two hundred years. Although the Inquisition struck terror into the hearts of the Goans; it did not affect the economic situation. Magnificent churches were constructed and *Cidade de Goa* came to be known as the *'Rome of the East'*.

In 1580, Portugal detested the arrival of the Spaniards and the Dutch into India, who threatened to deprive the Portuguese of their prized possessions. Dutch ships and African pirates often attacked the Portuguese galleys mid sea and took off with their valuable cargo. Portugal lost many of her best warships in this tussle for supremacy of the trade route.

Over land, the Portuguese were constantly troubled by the Marathas under Shivaji, the great Maratha warrior and king, who made many forays into Portuguese territories from the North.

It is against this backdrop that young Paula set foot on Goan soil.

Chapter 1

CARREIRA D' INDIA
(Sea route to India)

The Bay of Mahajanga in northwestern Madagascar lay basking in the silvery light of early dawn. The water was absolutely calm; making it appear like an immense lake. A few fishing boats could be seen playing hide and seek in the morning mist. But further out at sea loomed a huge silhouette of a Portuguese galley. The strange black flag atop the main mast carried an emblem with an allegory of freedom—two hands with broken chains, which meant, 'freedom'. Painted proudly on the prow, in bold letters was the name *'Trovão'* which meant thunder, in Portuguese. It had seen many victories when it was a warship with the Portuguese navy, engaging the Dutch ships along the lucrative trade route to India and the Far East. It was in one such fight that the ship got separated from the rest after the Dutch boarded it, killing almost all sailors on board except for the African slaves below deck. Out of those who survived from among its crew, were a young officer named Sergio and his close friend Algernon, a deserter from the French navy who seized the opportunity to take command of the ship. Sergio was unanimously selected as the captain of the ship whilst Algernon became the ship's mate.

During this time, a trans-Saharan trading network had been launched to transport slaves up north. The discovery of new lands in the east by the Portuguese had created a great demand for slaves for use in farming, mining and other domestic tasks in their newly created colonies.

Sergio and Algernon were totally against the concept of slavery and frustrated the Portuguese traders who undertook such a beastly trade. They wanted to be known as pirates who fought for humanity and not mere treasure.

Before deciding to settle in the Bay of Mahajanga in Madagascar and establishing a small community of white and black settlers there, they had garnered support from the King of Mohili, one of the islands of the Comoros that was in constant war with the inhabitants of Anjouan, another of the islands. The Comoros consisted of four volcanic islands in the Indian Ocean situated between mainland Africa and Madagascar. Sergio and Algernon had banished slavery on their settlement and schooled the blacks in the principles of freedom.

Nestling atop a green plateau, the sleepy cottages stirred awake with life as the women of the house arose to light their stoves for breakfast. As chimneys spewed coffee scented smoke that mingled with the aroma of freshly baked bread, Captain Sergio opened the window shutters of his study and breathed in, the fresh morning air. He was a tall, rugged man. His battle-scarred face and muscular body made him appear fierce and cruel, but at heart he was a true gentleman, a fact well recognized by his loyal crew. Looking over the ever—spreading settlement that he and his dear friend Algernon had created, the twinkle in his bright blue eyes could only mean that he was very pleased. His mission in life had been accomplished. They had even created their own coded language, borrowing words from African, French, English, Dutch, Portuguese and Malagasy languages. The pirates preyed on the slave ships, recruiting the human cargo to their own cause and clothing them and instructing them in the arts of sailing and navigation.

In the several attacks that Sergio and his men had carried out on the Portuguese ships that plied the spice route, scores of slaves were released and housed on the island settlement. Many of the freed slaves were reunited with their loved ones who had been given up for dead.

The harbour was large and protected enough to hide the *Trovao* and numerous other smaller ships that the pirates had captured. The bay was also ideally located for launching raids on Portuguese ships on their way to Indian coasts or heading home to Portugal. As Captain Sergio's gaze finally rested on the beach below, he noticed Abdul and Jafar, two Ghanaian fishermen from his community, trundling up the rugged pathway that led up to his house at the edge of a rocky outcrop, overlooking the bay.

"*Capitao! Capitao!* Portuguese galleon and three '*naus*' spotted at sea!" shouted out Abdul excitedly.

"The galleon . . . *muito grande, senhor*", said Jaffar, gesticulating wildly.

"Send word to our ship's council that we are meeting on board the *Trovão* soon after breakfast. We must decide quickly whether to risk an attack or not, specially if we are going to be outweighed", said Captain Sergio decisively.

... ঌ ♦ ঌ ...

The *Trovão's* deck was abuzz with news of the Portuguese ships. The description of the ships if accurate meant only one thing—it had to be full of slaves. The ten council members were hardy sailors, always ready for action. There were five who were Africans who never wasted a single opportunity to free their suffering brethren. Captain Sergio and Algernon soon appeared on the upper deck and greeted each of the ten men.

"*Meus amigos*, you must have heard about the Portuguese ships out there . . . . What do we do?" asked Captain Sergio.

"Judging by the size of the galleon that the fishermen spoke of, it appears that a large number of slaves are being taken to their Indian colonies. And . . . if we attack, we will suffer a lot of casualties and sure defeat", responded Luis. As head of the council, Luis knew from previous battles at sea for the same worthy cause, how the outcome could swing in favour of the enemy without the required numbers and fire power.

"What we need once again, is a plan. A plan that will take the enemy by surprise and give us enough time to relieve them of their human cargo", said Algernon, opening a map and laying it down on a wooden crate.

Sergio was known to be a good strategist. He scanned the map closely and then using his dagger as a pointer, traced the Mozambique Channel with its point. The Portuguese had found the conditions in Mozambique reasonably good for agriculture with the humid tropical climate, high temperatures and rainfall in the north. Also, the locals fished for lobster and shrimp, which was well desired by the Portuguese. Madagascar on its opposite shores was sparsely populated and there were more cattle on the large island than humans! The central part was made up of high Savanna-covered plateaus and in the east, forested mountains fell steeply to the coast with the southwestern side falling gradually through grassland and scrub. Only five percent of the land was cultivated and the produce sufficed only its natives.

"We cannot engage them in this channel as the Portuguese presence in Mozambique and the fortifications along the coast will immediately come to their rescue", he observed.

Then, pointing at the open waters just outside the Channel and to the north of Madagascar, he punctured the map with such force that all the others who were peering excitedly at the map, jumped back with a start.

"*Então!*" we scatter them here and attack the galleon with *Trovão!*"

Then turning to Habib, the dark giant from the Gold Coast, he said, "Organize the three small sail ships we captured from the Muslim traders and fit them out with four canons each with enough ammunition to lead the '*naus*' away from the galleon. Luis, Habib and Abdul will captain the sail ships whilst I lead you with the *Trovão*. We shall go out tonight and anchor at the Devil's Cove at the north of the island and put a watch at the highest point on the Comoros Islands. We will attack upon their signal. All lamps shall be put out. The sail ships shall leave first and engage the three trailing 'naus'. Whilst you slow them down with your surprise attack, *Trovão* will take on the galleon. Let us hope that the operation will be swift and bloodless. Now go! Prepare for battle!"

As was the usual custom, Sergio, Algernon and a few others stood in a ring holding hands and looking up to the heavens, praying for God's protection.

The good pirates set sail towards the Comoros. The Indian monsoon winds from the north usually made the weather treacherous during the months of November to April, accompanied by cyclones, but fortunately for them, the rough season was just over. Upon reaching the heavily forested tropical islands, the pirates cast their anchors in a sheltered bay and sent out a couple of men, suitably equipped to signal the arrival of the Portuguese from above the highest point of the island.

Although it was new moon, billions of stars of varying brilliance punctuated the infinite vastness of the ethereal heavens. The ocean was surprisingly calm, and little wavelets rose and fell, making gentle lapping sounds. The pin-drop silence of the night was sweetly disturbed by the sound of percussion instruments and fiddles which came from a big sea vessel that was darkly silhouetted against the starry night. It was the 'Santa Barbara', the large multi-decked ship, surrounded with 30 demi-cannon ports.

The hurricane lamps around the deck highlighted the joyful faces of the musicians and the dancers. Three graceful couples whirled and swirled around each other to the foot tapping 'corridinho' rhythm of a famous Portuguese folk song. The flapping sound of their colourful skirts seemed to complement the sound of the ship's white sails carried on five masts of sturdy pine. The *Santa Barbara* was powered entirely by sails. The drumming of the dancers' feet on the fairly new timber boards of the ship's deck, as they performed the triple hop-step of the 'O *corridinho*' dance, seemed to reverberate all the way down to the ship's hold that was fitted with precious cargo of silver and fine cloth which would be traded for gold and spices, much valued in the west. Returning ships usually carried twice the amount of silver in gold, precious stones and spices. The young ladies appeared to be in their teens and danced spiritedly with their handsome young partners. The lady, who was dancing with an older gentleman, attracted admiring glances from the dreamy eyes of the young sailors, who had their gaze fixed on her countenance, their minds conjuring up images of romantic liaisons with her.

"Bravo young lady, you are a glorious dancer, indeed", applauded the elderly man dressed in colours of the king's army, the military uniform showing off his high bearing.

Overhearing the complement, a man whose epaulettes on his uniform revealed that he was the captain of the ship remarked, "That's our Paula. She was the apple of her father's eye. I wish he was alive to take this trip with his daughter".

Paula blushed at the attention she was receiving from all around. The soft light of the hurricane lamps made her supple complexion glow like pearls and the flickering flame reflected in her aquamarine blue eyes seemed to keep time with her two plaits of blonde hair, bouncing merrily over the small of her back. She looked strikingly beautiful in her colourful flair skirt and silk blouse that offset the floral patterns of her embroidered vest. Although lean and delicate in structure, her resolve was written all over her face. Her priorities in life were well arranged, just like the timber carvels strongly joined to the robust skeleton of the ship.

The long, narrow Galleon was being followed by three 'naus'. Unlike the Santa Barbara, which had a square stern, the naus had round tuck sterns. They also differed in their arrangement of masts and sails. The Galleon held the lead, with its snout projected a great distance forward from the bows, below the level of the forecastle, very much like a sword pointed towards the enemy by a charging general in battle. Except . . . there was no enemy in sight.

As Paula's partner whirled her around, arm in arm, the great white sails above them billowed and flapped in the strong wind pushing the galleon speedily across the ocean, away from the Iberian peninsula and onward to the great African Coast.

...ॐ✦ॐ...

The *Santa Barbara* had left the port on the Tagus River in Lisbon on March 29, 1667. The journey to Goa, one of Portugal's prime colonies, would take them southward around the Cape of Good Hope and roughly northward up the East African Coast, close to the coast of Mozambique. There would be short stopovers at small trading posts of Angouche, Sofala and '*Ilha de Mozambique*', before continuing on a north-westerly route towards the Horn of Africa, and turning eastwards past the Arabian Peninsula and then to the coast of India.

Besides the precious cargo of silver, porcelain and the fabrics, the captain of the Santa Barbara had something even more precious to protect! Under his charge were a top military general and the three young beautiful ladies. In fact, protecting the ladies was giving him sleepless nights. It was not just the fear of storms or pirates but he had to keep his own men at bay!

...ॐ✦ॐ...

Back in the spacious cabin below deck, Clara and Linda were fast asleep. The merriment on the deck and exposure to the cold earlier that evening had taken its toll on the young ladies, who had retired to bed straight after supper.

They were orphans who were under the direct protection of the King. Such orphans were called *'Orfaas Del Rei'*. Usually, these were daughters of Portuguese soldiers and sailors who were killed on duty and there was no one to pay the exorbitant dowries. So the King took them under his wing and sent them to the colonies at his expense to be married to Portuguese men when they came of age. In Goa, the *Santa Casa de Misericóórdia* or the Holy House of Mercy was a social organization which was set up on the lines of a smaller institution in Portugal, initiated by Queen Eleanor the wife of King Joao II and sister of King Manuel I, who became king after her husband's death. She was extremely wealthy, and used her money for charity. In 1498, she had spearheaded the creation of various *Santa Casa da Misericórdia*, as confraternities with humanitarian purposes, especially the care of the poor, the sick, and abandoned children. More institutions were founded in other towns and cities of Portugal and in the Portuguese colonies. In Goa, they looked after the *Orfaas Del Rei*. The *Senado* (Municipal Council) also looked after them.

The Captain had requested Paula, who was a few years older than the orphans, to keep an eye on them. A slave girl named Theresa, who was also traveling with them, was ordered to take care of all their housekeeping needs on board the ship. The Captain knew Paula since she was a child. In fact, her father Henri Menezes was his former superior. They had been on several voyages together and he was only too willing to carry out the request of Paula's widowed mother.

Paula put down her diary after making another entry into it and gazed at the two orphans. "How unfortunate not to have parents", she thought to herself.

Her father had meant everything to her and she could not imagine growing up without him. His loss was unbearable and although Paula loved her mother very much, she had decided to act upon her father's words—"My dearest Paula", he had once said to her, "If you ever want to see heaven without dying, you must visit Goa".

Ever since that day, she had yearned to visit Goa. And here she was, burning inwardly with passion, braving dangerous waters to fulfill that wish. She had decided to pen each and every event worth recording, in her thick leather-bound diary. This diary would be a testimony of her experience in Goa for all generations to come in her family. She wished that each and every member of her family would be inspired by her writing, to visit Goa and experience the 'heaven on earth' that her father had experienced.

Paula was a voracious reader who loved to follow Portuguese maritime achievements through the accounts of great Portuguese explorers of the 15th and 16th centuries. Although she was tired, she coaxed her sleepy eyes to complete just one more chapter in the book that she had borrowed from the captain. This book was fascinating in its details of the maritime history and records of maps and routes charted by the great explorers like Albuquerque, Da Gama and Magellan. Paula was only interested in those chapters that spoke of Goa. She had decided that for the next two or three years of her life, all she wanted to do was fill her life with every detail of Goa.

The book she had opened was titled *'Carreira d'India'*. Everything about Portugal's great navigators and their achievements was recorded—from Prince Henri 'The Navigator', son of King John I, who acquired African territory for Portugal through his navigators in the 15th century, to circumnavigation of the Cape of Good Hope by Bartolomeu Dias in 1488 and later by Vasco Da Gama in 1498, sailing further up the East coast of Africa, touching Sofala and Malindi and landing in India. Although it made Paula proud of the great achievements of these brave seafarers, it saddened her heart to learn that Portugal engaged heavily in the lucrative business of slave trading. The previous day, she had stopped reading the book at this point because she was greatly troubled over this fact.

Tonight, as she resumed her reading, the pages flew as she got very engrossed in the voyages made by Alfonso de Albuquerque in 1503 onwards. It was he who was the first to conduct trade with India and together with his cousin Francisco de Almeida, set up a fortress and trading post at the kingdom of Cochin and then Quilon. He then returned in 1506 at the order of King Manuel, to capture the islands of Socotra and Ormuz, thereby controlling the trade via the Red Sea, the gateway to all sea routes at that time. In 1510, he decided to fight the kingdom of Cochin but was defeated. He had then focused his attention on Goa, then ruled by Sultan Adil Shah of Bijapur.

Once again, Paula broke into tears when she read how Alfonso de Albuquerque massacred Muslims, desecrated mosques and destroyed Muslim institutions, when he re-stormed Goa after being pushed out by Adil Shah's forces with the help of Timoja, a Hindu captain and his flotilla of 23 ships.

She rushed upstairs into the chilly night sobbing uncontrollably and repeating, "Why, oh why did Albuquerque have to kill innocent people?"

As the cool wind caressed her silky black hair and filled her nostrils with the salty odour, Paula's mind raced back to happier memories, to a beach near Lisbon . . .

It was late that evening. A luminous moon was dominating the star-studded skies. But the fiery orange flames of a campfire outshone its cool white light. A small group of men and women, young and old were sitting around it. A sweet mature voice was passionately singing what sounded like a love song. But it was not in Portuguese. In fact, the instrument accompanying the song was as alien as the language! It was a '*ghumot*', a round earthen pot with animal skin stretched across two openings.

"Come now Paula, dance those steps I taught you. After all, you will not be among us two days from now", persuaded the singer during a musical interlude. It was an elderly lady with a compassionate voice; her hair neatly tied into a bun behind her head. At that, a girl of about ten years of age approached Paula shyly and attempted to pull her up from where she was sitting in the sand.

"Paula, please teach me the dance that *Avozinha* taught you. I thought you liked the beat of the *ghumot*", the young lass cajoled.

Paula gave in to the pleas of her little neighbour Helena, whom she adored. As she danced to the beat of the slow, graceful melody, the sound of the *ghumot* seemed to grow louder and louder until her reverie was rudely disturbed by a harsh, jarring noise, which was accompanied by a splintering crash! The ship shuddered violently, knocking her against the heavy timber balustrade of the deck.

It didn't take Paula long to realize that they had been hit by a canon ball. "Oh, my God! I think we are being attacked!" exclaimed Paula, as she tore down the steps, leading to her quarters. When she reached below deck, the ship rocked violently and remained tilted at a precarious angle for a few seconds. Paula struggled to maintain her balance. Recovering quickly from the shock of the impact, her mind was now focused on the safety of Clara and Linda. Ever since Paula had met them, she had felt a sense of responsibility towards them. She barged inside the room, face taut with anxiety. Linda sat bundled up in a corner, shivering uncontrollably. Clara was nowhere to be seen.

"Where is Clara?" she screamed, praying that the young girl was safe.

"Sh . . . sh . . . she had gone to the toilet with Theresa and I fear for her safety", she sobbed.

Paula was quaking with shock; however, she quickly composed herself enough not to show it outwardly. Concern for Clara galvanized her into action. She made the sign of the Cross and left Linda's side, to go out and look for Clara but Linda hung onto her arm.

"Linda, you are safe here. Do not be afraid. Trust in Jesus. Engage the crossbar behind the door after I have left and do not open it for anyone except for the Captain and for me", she told the frightened girl as calmly as she could.

Slowly disengaging her arm and taking the scared girl's hand in hers, she said nervously, "I will see where the girls are".

As she came out of the cabin, she met a frightened Theresa, gesticulating wildly, "No go out, missy!! Fire . . . fire . . . boom . . . boom!!" Bad men attack ship!!"

"Calm down, Theresa, and tell me where Clara is", Paula implored. "Missy . . . . missy . . . Cl . . . Cl . . . Clara fall in sea!!" Theresa replied, with eyes wide open in shock.

But before Theresa could say anything further, there was another loud crash and the sound of breaking wood filled the air. Soon, they heard the shouts and screams of men in combat, along with the sound of metal striking metal.

. . . ❧◆❦ . . .

Theresa waited patiently with a candle for Clara to come out of the toilet. She was tired from the chores of the day. Although she was a slave girl, the three ladies on the ship were treating her very well. She particularly loved Paula who she admired not only for her beauty but also for her kindness. No one had treated a poor slave girl the way she had. Although young, Paula was almost like a mother to the teenage girls. Theresa was happy that she had been deputed to look after the needs of the three ladies and hoped that she would strive to be in their service even after they would leave the ship in Goa. Theresa gradually dozed off in a corner of the vestibule area of the toilet, but her reverie was short-lived as the whole side of the ship which Clara was occupying, disappeared from her sight in a deafening explosion that threw splinters and water barrels up in the air. The whole ship shuddered with the impact. The last she heard of Clara was her terrified screams as she disappeared into the darkness of the night. After the initial shock of the situation settled down, Theresa composed herself and raced down the dimly lit corridor of the ship's quarter's screaming hysterically.

For five long days, the pirates lay in wait at the Comoros islands for the Portuguese to emerge from the long Mozambique Channel.

On the sixth evening just as the sun was retiring for the night, the scouts at the top of the hill signaled with flame torches. All four of the scouts, atop the main masts of the ships, also sighted the Portuguese ships, "four ships on the horizon", they warned from above.

As planned, the three smaller sail ships waited until dark and proceeded towards the Portuguese, keeping a safe distance from them. Not a single light was burning on board. Being a new moon night, the whole ocean was steeped in darkness. The sails of the three pirate ships flapped in unison making a great noise. But soon each one gained a safe distance from each other and the noise dissipated. The men were busy preparing the canons for the action that was to begin in a few minutes time. The three sail ships carried fewer men, as fighting was not at all anticipated. Their mission was to lure the three Portuguese *naus* into leaving the galleon exposed to an attack by their Captain and his fighters. The *Trovão* had at least a hundred men on the mission, their role in the attack was to board the galleon and free the slaves on board.

As per the instructions of their own captains, they were to hold fire until the *Trovão* had fired the first shot at the galleon. As the *Trovão* inched closer and closer to the dimly lit galleon, sweet music of fiddles and percussion instruments came wafting through the breeze. They were having some kind of a celebration on the deck. The Captain ordered his men to slow down the approach.

Turning to his companion, he said, "Let us not spoil their merriment. And, after all, drunken men cannot fight. It will be to our advantage to let them have their fill".

"Bravo Captain! You are brilliant. What would we do without you?" They chorused.

The Captain and his mate, along with the other pirates waited, amused with the free entertainment provided by the Portuguese. After what appeared to be an eternity, the musicians seemed to be winding down as they starting playing tunes at slow tempo. Soon the activity on the deck seemed to diminish. It was at this point when Sergio ordered the first salvo of canon fire on the galleon. They were about 200 meters away from the square 'tuck stern'. The force of the impact tore a huge gap into the corner of the mammoth ship. As splinters and wood planks flew into the sky, the cloud of white smoke momentarily screened the Galleon. A single high-pitched scream of a lady shattered the lull which followed the first salvo, only to be drowned by another shot from the portside cannons, this time through the mizzen mast.

The Captain ordered his men to stand-by to ram the ship and board it. The expert helmsman made a slight adjustment to the bearing of the *Trovão* and set its course to ram the Galleon mid side. The pirates braced themselves for the impact. Both ships seemed to shudder with the shock. The sound of splintering wood filled the night sky. Soon after the impact, the *Trovão* was ingeniously swung around to align itself with the galleon. More cannon shots were fired by the other pirate ships which had now come upon the other trailing *naus*. The fight was very much on as planned. The name 'Santa Barbara' was at least a couple of meters above the *Trovão's* prow.

"Throw up the ropes and nets, and scale the sides quickly. Kill only if necessary", Sergio ordered.

"Get back in!" shouted a concerned man, yelling from atop the stairs, "Pirates have boarded our ship. Stay indoors and lock yourselves in!" he added.

Paula recognized the voice as that belonging to the young officer who had danced with Linda the previous evening. Though she looked very fragile, Paula had nerves of steel. Perhaps it was concern for Clara's safety, which made her that way. Whatever it was, the young lady did not follow the young officer's advice as she ran towards the well-decorated corridor of the officer's deck where her quarters were located, and encountered the elderly general and a few officers with drawn cutlasses stomping down the corridor towards her. They had been caught completely unawares by the happenings above. Their men needed leaders and they had realized that. Being hardcore army and navy men, they were going to join their valiant men on deck, in their fight against the pirates.

Paula quietly stepped inside an open room and hid behind the door till they had passed. Had the general seen her walking around the corridor, he would have locked her into her room permanently, knowing full well the danger a pretty woman would be in, if caught by the pirates. Tip-toeing out of the room and hoping not to encounter any more of the ship's men, she raced back to the toilet block. It was steeped in darkness, and strangely, through the back of an open toilet cubicle, she could see the night sky. A million stars appeared to be twinkling ever so fiercely, almost warning her not to step any closer because a few feet away from her, the whole floor and wall had been blown away by the pirates, leaving a gaping hole in the stern of the ship. Paula felt her knees weaken and slowly sank towards the floor sobbing bitterly. "Oh Clara, I hope you are alive and safe".

Heartbroken and dazed by what she had seen, Paula walked slowly back towards her quarters, She stood outside her door, dreading to break the sad news to Linda and Theresa. Lacking the courage to do so, she walked slowly towards the stairs leading up to the deck, listening to the yells of charging men and groans of those who were injured. Suddenly, she froze in fright as she heard heavy labored breathing sounds, accompanied by groans of someone in pain. Lying sprawled across the floor, with blood oozing profusely from a deep gash in the side of his head, was a dark skinned man, who had been badly injured in the fighting. As their eyes met, the pirate moaned and opened his mouth, indicating that he was thirsty. Her heart filled with pity, she rushed to the barrel of drinking water, which was kept in a corner and filled the dipper with water. But as she was about to take it to the wounded pirate, a young officer vaulted over the handrail of the stair and came between Paula and the pirate, with his cutlass drawn, "Stay back, *Senhora*! That man is dangerous", he screamed.

Sensing his concern, Paula who was momentarily rooted to the spot, ran forward and sidestepped the young officer and stood between him and the pirate.

"Sir, that man is not dangerous. He is wounded and needs water!" she told him firmly and calmly, surprised at her own courage.

"But, *Senhora*, he will not hesitate to kill . . ."

Not waiting to let him finish his warning, she gathered her skirt and knelt beside the wounded pirate and carefully emptied the water into his open mouth by supporting his bleeding head with her left hand.

"*asante . . . asante*", he said smiling.

"Yes, *kamratra*", she said, slowly lowering his head onto the floor. His eyes appeared to be drooping and the movement in his hands and feet had stopped. The grip on her hand had loosened and his hand was now lying motionless. His eyes seemed to focus on hers, unblinking; a smile of gratitude etched across his face. He had breathed his last.

The officer stood transfixed, watching all that had just happened. His eyes were full of admiration for Paula. He reacted just in time to hold Paula as she fainted. The stress and the exertion had finally taken its toll on her.

Only a few aboard the *Santa Barbara* had managed to react to the situation and had armed themselves with cutlasses and pistols. Even as they made their way hurriedly to the deck from their quarters, many sailors were so drunk from the earlier celebrations that they were totally useless.

There was fierce fighting on the deck. Cutlass met cutlass and pistol shots were accompanied with screams of pain. There was blood everywhere and men from both sides lay moaning and writhing in pain.

The pirate Captain screamed at his men, "Why aren't the slaves released yet?"

Three of his pirates appeared from below the deck through the hatches, "Captain, there are no slaves on this ship except fabric and other cargo".

The Captain saw that the crew and officers of the *Santa Barbara* were slowly increasing in numbers on the deck. Two elderly gentlemen had joined the fight in the uniform of a naval captain and an army general. One of them was heading straight for him.

Taking a high guard, the general came charging at the pirate chief, bringing his cutlass down on his head like an axe about to strike a block of wood. The Captain sidestepped the blow and swung his cutlass sideways ripping the general's garment at his arm and drawing blood and a painful exclamation. But the general was not giving up. Just as he was steadying himself for a counter blow, Algernon's voice seemed to boom across the deck. "Retreat, retreat back to the ship. There are no slaves here . . . just sailors and women! Retreat!"

The Captain had once again anticipated the general's move and had cleverly sidestepped and tripped him down. He raised his weapon to finish the general off, but instead, looked into the general's stunned face and said", I am Captain Sergio, the leader of the pirates. We came to release slaves but you don't seem to have any. Therefore, we will spare you. *Boa noite*".

And so saying, Captain Sergio was over and down the side of the Santa Barbara in a flash. The other men followed suit. The *Trovão* was already moving away from the side of the Santa Barbara. A few pistol shots were fired at them from above but a sharp order, which appeared to come from the general, appeared to have calmed the defenders onboard the Santa Barbara. Two great men had met and fought each other and left each other with a rare kind of respect only warriors could comprehend.

Whilst all this was happening, Clara was battling for her life.

"Help! Help me . . . . Please!" cried out Clara desperately, hoping that someone on *Santa Barbara* would hear her and come to her rescue, but to no avail. The two ships were engaged in the thick of battle, canons blazing. The icy chill of the Indian Ocean made Clara freeze all over. She had to find something fast to climb onto. It was pitch dark out there. The ships had put out all their lights trying to make it difficult to spot each other. As she frantically thrashed about in the water, she grimaced with pain as her arm struck something flat and hard. Clara's hopes were raised, but her joy only lasted a few seconds as she discovered that the plank of wood was too small to carry her weight.

"There must be a whole floor of the lavatory floating somewhere around here", she thought as she remembered how the rear of the ship had suddenly opened up, taking away the main supports of the toilet floor, causing her to be thrown off the ship. She swam in a large circle hoping to find her 'raft' somewhere. Slowly, her energy waned and she floated on her back, looking up at the starry skies. "This is it, dear God; I am ready to come to you. I can't survive like this", she closed her eyes and let the sea, bob her gently to sleep. Just then, the creaking of timber nearby awakened her and filled her with hope once again. Clara slowly paddled painstakingly towards the sound. Every move she made was sending excruciating waves of pain to her head. At last, she was holding the splintered edge of a large plank of wood. With every ounce of will power and strength, Clara hauled herself up and rolled over onto the plank . . . . And this time it held! To her good fortune, she had found the raft she was looking for. Clara bundled up into a tight coil, shivering incessantly. If God had provided a raft, he would also provide her something to keep her safe from the cold wind. As she lay coiled on her raft, her foot suddenly felt something soft. Puzzled as to what it could be, she rose to a sitting position and touched the spot when she had felt the fabric. Carefully dislodging it from the rough edge of her raft, she started pulling the rest of the fabric on board. It was a part of a sail but large enough to make her a windshield! It took Clara ages to wring the fabric as dry as she possibly could. And covering herself with the damp sailcloth, Clara said a prayer for all the wonderful people on board the *Santa Barbara*, whose fate was as unclear as hers, and closed her eyes commending her life into the hands of God.

...❧◆❧...

"Where am I? Give the man water . . ." muttered Paula, slipping in and out of consciousness.

"Ah . . . . at last, my brave lady awakes", said the ship's doctor jovially, "I think a few more women like you would have transformed the world into a peaceful one".

Paula gave him a pale smile. Her eyes wandered around the room. She was lying in her bunk bed inside her cabin. Theresa was seated by her head, holding a sponge to her face whilst Linda caressed her feet at the other end of the bed.

"*Obrigado doutor.* Have we reached Goa yet?"

"Not yet, dear. For the time being, we have anchored off the coast of Malindi, in Africa. The ship is undergoing repairs. She is getting a new mast fitted and the stern is being boarded up".

The mention of the damages to the ship's stern suddenly brought tears to her eyes as she remembered Clara.

Limbering herself up and looking at Linda, she asked, "Did you manage to find Clara? Please tell me she is fine", she implored.

The question remained unanswered. All she got was silence and sad, tearful glances.

"Cla . . . ra is still missing . . . the . . . the . . . they say she must have fallen overboard during the shelling of the stern", said Linda nervously.

Theresa had not dared to wait for Clara to get out of the toilet as she had fled to get help after the shell had hit the stern.

Paula was filled with immense sorrow and could not speak after that. Grief-stricken and desiring the journey to end quickly, she asked Captain Joao dejectedly, "When will we be in Goa, Captain?"

"Very soon, dear", said the Captain. "Soon we shall be leaving Malindi for Goa". He squeezed Paula's hand reassuringly.

Soon after the pirates had left the *Santa Barbara* badly crippled without its mizzen mast and part of the stern ripped out, Captain Joao had decided to wait till morning to regroup with the three *naus* that were not responding to his fire signals. It appeared that they had been scattered by the pirates on purpose, as they would have attempted to come to their rescue.

By the first light of dawn, the three *naus* had been reunited with the mother ship. Their officers had carried out an inspection of each ship's exterior and it was decided that before proceeding to Goa across the Indian Ocean, it would be better to get the ships repaired. Malindi in Kenya was the obvious choice since the Portuguese had a trading post there.

...❧♦❧...

Chapter 2

CIDADE DE GOA
(City Of Goa)

———— ৵ ৵ ————

Paula sat quietly watching the sunrise from the direction of Goa. She had been up early that day. For the last month or so, she had been pining for the day when she would at last, set foot on the glorious shores of Goa. The repairs of the ship were completed and its holds were being stocked with fruit, yam, salted dried meat and water. As she watched the slaves bringing in the supplies with their sweat-soaked, sunburnt bodies glistening in the light of the rising sun, she wished freedom for them and wondered when the sun would stop setting on them. The more she thought about slavery, the more it sickened her to the stomach. To think that her country had taken on the role of evangelization of new lands, with a religion that taught equality! The kings, nobility and the merchants were following their own gospel of convenience. Even religious institutions of the time could not do without the use of slaves! Paula hated this hypocrisy that existed in the Church and whilst she loved Christ and His teachings, she hated the inhumanity supported by the church.

As she reflected on this unfair trade, her thoughts wandered off to Portugal and her dear nanny Catherine De Souza. Catherine was 80 years of age and had been Paula's father's faithful nanny; now an integral part of their family in Portugal.

"Oh Catherine, how I miss you!" Paula sighed. She closed her eyes and felt the presence of the dear old lady right next to her—silky brown hair with just a smattering of grey, wheat brown skin and a rich smile which showed off her *joie-de-vivre*. It was she who had cultivated wanderlust in Paula and made her artistic soul yearn for the beautiful land that she spoke of with such nostalgia and love. The images Catherine conjured up with words, made Paula feel as though she had lived in Goa herself. To compliment this talent, Catherine had a great hand at embroidery and had completed many landscapes.

"Catherine could have been such a great poetess, if only she had the right education", thought Paula, "I could actually imagine the swaying palms and the wind playing with their fronds. I could hear the waves crashing onto the shell-strewn golden sands of the long and snaky coastline, as Catherine described the place".

Catherine was deeply dedicated to the Menezes family who loved her and treated her as their own. She had a flair for languages and could speak English, Portuguese and Swahili, besides her native Konkani which she tried to teach Paula, in preparation for her trip to Goa.

Catherine knew this would happen sooner or later, when Henri would take his family there at least for a holiday.

Catherine was a third generation Roman Catholic, whose grandfather was converted by St. Francis Xavier himself, who came to Goa in 1542. She was only 8 when her father died and at age 15, she had lost her dear mother. During that time, her sister Lucy who was working for the Abranches household in the village of Oddavel had arranged a job in the house of Colonel Diogo de Menezes, who had come to Goa as an emissary of the Portuguese King. He was newly married and his wife, who groomed her and taught her to speak Portuguese, at once liked Catherine. Diogo was very good to the locals and this was something which his superior in Portugal didn't like. Just three years after taking up his post in Goa, he was called back to Portugal. His wife had persuaded him to take Catherine with them and Catherine, who had nothing to lose in life by this decision, accepted to go to Portugal with them.

Paula recollected how Catherine was saddened to see her go. Somehow, she had made her feel like it was the last time they would see each other. She remembered that last blessing Catherine had given her in front of a statue of the Blessed Virgin Mary. She was deeply devoted to the Virgin Mary and was a keen follower of Christ. "My child, go forth fearlessly, knowing that Jesus is always with you. As long as you lead an honest and pure life, God and the whole universe will be on your side. What you sow in God's kingdom you will surely reap as a rich harvest". Later she had told her about her nephew Pedro who was working for Captain Lino, whose wife Paula was going to serve as a lady-in-waiting. Catherine had already written to Pedro about Paula and Catherine knew that he and his wife Ana would love to look after her. Sadly, Pedro and Ana had lost their teenage daughter to drowning a couple of years ago.

Paula now looked forward to her meeting with Pedro and Ana. It wasn't going to be too bad after all! She was sure to be in safe and loving hands with anyone connected to Catherine's family.

Her thoughts were disturbed by the Captain's baritone voice startling her back to the present, "And what are you so pensive about? Cheer up! Tomorrow morning we expect a good wind to buffet our sails and off we will go across the Indian Ocean to Goa!"

"*Bom dia*, Captain, I was only missing my mother and all the lovely people who I've left behind. It will be a long while before we see them again".

"I wish I had more time to talk to your dear mother that day at the port in Belem. You had arrived just as the boys were lifting the heavy barrels of gunpowder onboard. Good thing we carried the ammunition, or else I cannot imagine what the pirates would have done to us!"

Paula's mind wandered back to Portugal . . .

It was early morning that day, at the busy port of Belem near Lisbon. The port was situated on the Tagus, close to the mouth of the river where it joined the Atlantic Ocean. Several large galleons and *naus* were busy getting stocked with provisions for long journeys to the Portuguese colonies in the east. Most of the smaller ships utilized for earlier expeditions were now replaced with larger, roomier ships carrying not only trade cargo, but also military personnel and civilians. The *Santa Barbara* was towering above all the other ships in the port. It was an impressive galleon, commissioned by the King himself. It was specially built to carry aristocrats and other dignitaries to Portuguese lands across the seas. In a week's time, she would depart on her maiden voyage to Goa or as it was rightfully called by the seafarers 'Pearl of the Orient', because of its incomparable beauty. As soon as Paula had been told of her selection for the job in Goa as lady-in-waiting to Dona Herodiana, the wife of Captain Lino, she had already made enquiries at the port to find out if there were any ships leaving for Goa, at that time. She remembered that day when she, accompanied by her mother Rosalia had visited the Santa Barbara's captain to request him to escort her to Goa. Rosalia's joy had known no bounds when she had realized that the Captain who greeted them was none other than Captain Joao Heredia, an old mate of her husband Henri. In fact, he had served under Henri on a couple of his voyages.

"Welcome aboard, Dona Rosalia, and this pretty lady must be Paula. How quickly children grow these days" 'he had remarked.

"Paula has been offered a job in Goa as lady-in-waiting to Dona Herodiana Abranches, wife of a captain in the Portuguese army in Goa", her mother had said.

To that he had commented, "Hmmm . . . I admire your courage Dona Rosalia and that of young Paula here. But I'm not sure whether you have made the right decision. Such a lovely girl would do well right here in Portugal"

"I know, Captain. But it was my late husband's desire for Paula to see Goa. She has an adventurous spirit and would like to experience life in her father's beloved Goa, at least for a couple of years. Besides, the nephew of our dear Catherine works for the same family", her mother had replied.

And here she was now sitting with Captain Joao on the Santa Barbara making the much-desired trip to Goa.

"I knew your father very closely. He was an honorable man who was truly in love with Goa. In fact, in our last voyage together, he had told me that he was waiting for the day when you would grow of age so that he could take you and your mother to Goa with him and settle there. So, Paula, you really wish to see the land which your father loved so much?" he asked Paula.

"I do, Sir! I wish to see the blue mountains and the sun-kissed beaches. I want to pluck the cashew-apples hanging on green trees. I want to smell the freshly cut hay and behold a hundred thousand fire-flies setting ablaze the mango tree in the monsoons", she replied with much passion.

"Wow, you are truly poetic, I must say. You are in for a treat, my girl", replied the Captain, captivated by the power of her words. "Now let me take your leave. I have to conduct an inspection of the stair to the hold. Captain Joao looked very elegant in his uniform. Paula remembered her own father in uniform. Henri had served as a captain on one of the King's galleons and had successfully completed a journey to Goa, Timor in Indonesia and Macau during his illustrious tenure. But Paula could enjoy her dad's company only till the age of 15. He had left a large void in their lives when he had passed away. Her mother Rosalia loved him very much and there was not a single week that passed during the past 5 years when she did not visit the local cemetery to pray at his tombstone. The cemetery was not far from their quaint old cottage at the foothill of the *Castel de St. Jorge* in Lisbon. An old ship's wheel hung on the gate in the picket fence that badly needed painting. On the wheel were carved three names—Henri, Rosalia and Paula.

Paula now thanked God, for all the happy years they had together. It was Rosalia her mother who had supported her in her wish to apply for the job at the Abranches. In anticipation of Paula leaving on her trip to Goa, her mother had already made arrangements to live with her brother who owned vineyards in the famous winegrowing region of Portugal - Porto. He had been living there since his wife had died. Being without children, he was leading a lonely existence. He was only too glad to have his sister around him.

What a happy feeling it was when the postman had arrived at their door, one fine morning, when Paula and Rosalia were having their usual *'Broa de Milho'* with coffee. Paula had rushed to the gate and the friendly postman had taken ages to find the envelope in his sachet. And when he did, he had pretended that he had made a mistake and had turned to walk away. How Paula's heart had sunk with disappointment! But then the postman had turned slowly and winked mischievously as he handed over the envelope to her. Paula had excitedly torn open the envelope as she raced to her mother, "*Mae, Mae*, it has come at last!" Immediately after, tears had rolled down her mother's cheeks. Paula had by then realized the full impact of this letter on her mother, but then Rosalia had said, "These are only tears of joy, my child. At last, your father's dream will come true!"

Captain Joao and the other sailors were by now well experienced with the wind systems in the Indian Ocean and the crossing towards the southern tip of India went off fairly smoothly compared to the rough and perilous journey that they had experienced since they had circumnavigated the Cape of Good Hope. The journey was well timed to avoid the monsoon wind system, which comprised of the strong northeast winds that blew from October to April. From May until October, south and west winds prevailed. In the Arabian Sea, violent monsoon brought rain to the Indian subcontinent. In a few days, they had reached Kanyakumari (Cape Camorin) in India. Even before the Portuguese had arrived in India, ocean trade routes had crossed the Arabian Sea since ancient times. Historically, sailors in a timber ship with a single sail called a *dhow* used the seasonal monsoon winds to cross the sea. The Arabian Sea also formed a part of the chief shipping route between Europe and

India via the Suez Canal, which linked the Red Sea with the Mediterranean Sea.

Keeping sight of the Malabar Coast of southern India, the *Santa Barbara* sailed onward towards the Konkan Coast of Central India along which was situated Goa. Of the many rivers that emptied themselves into the Arabian Sea, the Mandovi and the Zuari were the main rivers that marked the entry into Goa.

As the ships entered the Mandovi River, lofty spires of whitewashed churches and other governmental buildings came into view. All the passengers and sailors crowded onto the deck to have a first look at the much talked about *'Cidade de Goa'*

"There's the Viceroy's arch, built by the great explorer, Alphonso de Albuquerque to commemorate his triumphant entry into Goa after the defeat of Adil Shah in 1510", said Captain Joao, pointing to the magnificent edifice along the right bank of the river. "The spire behind the arch, over to the right, is that of the Cathedral of Santa Catarina, also built by Alphonso. A little beyond it, is the *Bom* Jesus Church, where now lie the canonized remains of Goa's patron saint, St. Francis Xavier". By now, almost every sailor and passenger was on deck, admiring the scene that unfolded in front of their very eyes.

Looking towards two palatial structures, the Captain's voice suddenly faded to almost a whisper as he described the building as 'Goa's most feared structure' called the

Palace of the Inquisition which stood right next to the Viceroy's Palace.

"Heretics and blasphemers of the faith are tried and sentenced to death there", he said softly. And then turning to the gathering on the deck, he said solemnly, "I hope none of you will have the misfortune of seeing the insides of that grotesque place. It is known to have the most gruesome torture chambers the world has ever seen!"

For a few seconds, there was total silence. Paula took a few nervous gulps thinking of what the Captain had just said. But she brushed those fearful thoughts aside and looked at the opposite bank at the verdant hills of Divar and other wooded landmasses behind it. A few local craft called *'tonna'* were plying the river carrying what appeared to be white sand, probably for the construction of new churches and stately houses along the banks of the river.

Just as Paula's gaze turned towards the right bank of the river, she caught the Captain's voice in mid-commentary *'The Rua Direita.'* he was saying, "is the most exciting of all streets in Goa. Unlike other streets in Goa, which were either quadrants or curved, this street continues straight unto the majestic church of Our Lady of Piety. The street is lined by massive stone buildings with curved doors topped by family crests of the *fidalgos* ".

As they neared the dock, Paula was awestruck by the animation of the place. There were beautifully decorated elephants with brown skinned natives, clad in loose white clothes from waist down. Officers of the Portuguese army, mounted on fine Arabian steeds trotted on the timber-lined dock. There were people of all kinds, Arabs, Indians and Chinese. African slaves carrying carved palanquins with their masters or mistresses, who had come to receive their goods or parcels, awaited the safe anchoring of the *Santa Barbara* and the three *naus*. The smaller boats to ferry the passengers and the cargo to shore, had already left the dock with natives and slaves pulling at the oars.

Paula had entered her cabin along with Theresa and Linda to gather their belongings, ready to set foot on the golden land of Goa. Everything that was said about Goa was turning out to be true . . .". Truly, Goa is heavenly", thought Paula as she smiled at Linda, who could only stare quizzically at her, not knowing what was on her mind.

"Sir, we are from the *Santa Casa de Misericordia de Goa*. We have come to receive the King's two orphans", said one of the two elderly ladies speaking to Captain Joao, who had accompanied them to the jetty.

The Holy House of Mercy was an institution formed to carry out the charitable projects like the hospital, which was started in 1547, which was called Hospital of All Saints. The Holy House of Mercy was later given charge over two houses namely, *Recolhimento do Nosa Senhora de Serra*, which was for orphans and *Recolhimento de Santa Maria Magdalena*—this was for women who had gone astray and wanted to atone for their evil way of life, and for widows. Only women between 14 and 30 were admitted. There were also paying lodgers called '*Donzellas*'—women whose husbands were away on duty. In the beginning, the *Santa Casa Da Misericordia de Goa* was pressurized to accommodate women whose husbands were out to kill them for their disloyalty!

The other lady from the Holy House of Mercy turned to Paula and Linda and asked, "Are these the two girls, Clara and Linda?" Captain Joao was quick to make the clarification to avoid Paula the discomfort of explaining Clara's disappearance.

"Only one of them is an *Orfa Del Rei*. This is Linda. I am deeply sorry that we lost Clara during a skirmish with some pirates. She fell overboard and by the time we started looking for her, it was too late. We could not find her. Let us hope and pray that she is safe".

"That is terrible and unfortunate! God protect her!" said the two ladies with tears in their eyes.

Taking Linda's arm, one of them said, "Come, my child, you have suffered enough". Then, turning to Theresa, the other lady commanded her to follow with the luggage.

Linda turned and ran into Paula's open arms and they both hugged each other for a long time, crying profusely. "Don't worry, Linda, I will always be there for you. I will definitely come to visit you when time permits. I will pray that you find a wonderful, loving husband", winked Paula mischievously.

Linda walked behind the two ladies, listening to their chatter. Feeling sorry for Theresa, who was struggling under the load of two bags, she took a piece of luggage from her. As she did that, a young and handsome officer who was passing them at that very moment murmured loud enough that she could hear—*"Admiravel"*. Their eyes met for a few seconds. They smiled at each other and continued on, sighing.

Paula's thoughts wandered off to her mother and *Avozinha* Catherine. She was already missing them but she felt her dead father's presence all around her. She felt a deep sense of peace engulf her. The thousands of miles from home did not intimidate her at all.

Her thoughts were disturbed by the sound of heavy boots on the timber. A uniformed man approached the general saluted him smartly and bowed to Paula. Paula continued with a smile.

"Sir, the Viceroy sends you his greetings. I am Lieutenant Mariano and I have been sent to escort you to the palace", he said.

"Thank you, Lieutenant", said the general returning his salute.

"Sir, your carriage is waiting", said Mariano.

"Good. But I will have to wait here till Captain Abranches and his wife arrive here to take charge of this young lady. I am sorry you will have to wait a while", said the General with a smile.

Lt. Mariano nodded to the General and said to Paula, "I have worked under Captain Lino's command several times. He is a wonderful person and you will enjoy working in his household".

Paula smiled warmly at him. "People in Portugal have spoken well of him. I am sure I will be fine there".

Captain Lino Abranches was sitting in his study brooding about what he had come to hear from his close friend Lieutenant Mariano just a few weeks back. It was all coming back to him now. He now knew why his wife was behaving very strangely with him. She definitely had a dark secret to hide. His attempts at convincing her to agree to have a baby were falling on deaf ears and the more he broached the topic, the more she abhorred him. Although his good conscience told him to break free from the recent bad habits he had fallen prey to, he felt helpless as he enslaved himself to alcohol and wild women. It was another of those horrible mornings, when he felt sick to the stomach from the late night of drinking and flirting. His head was exploding and every part of his body felt like it was falling apart. He was so drowsy that he didn't even hear the knock on his door. Not bothering to lift the sheets from his face, he said in a drunken voice, "Come in".

It was his trusted valet, Pedro, a tall, dark and rugged man. Although wiry in structure, his body was packed with muscles bulging through his vest. At the age of **55**, he was still agile and strong.

"Senhor, we have a messenger from the harbour. Dona Paula has arrived", said Pedro.

"Pedro, I thought senhora was going to the docks with you to receive her? Why are you bothering me? Go tell senhora", said Captain Lino in an irritated voice.

"I beg your pardon sir, but Dona Herodiana is resting in her room, Senhora".

The Captain struggled to lift himself up on one elbow, obviously annoyed but controlled. "Thank you, Pedro, I will go and check what happened. Maybe she forgot all about it!" he said, trying to sound as kind as possible although he was seething with rage.

After staggering to his wife's door and knocking for a long while, she at last opened the door.

"Herodiana honey, your lady-in-waiting is waiting", he said, disguising his irritation and making light of the situation, "I thought you were going to receive her?"

"Cut that out, Lino! I do not think it proper for me to go and receive my lady-in-waiting", she said pompously, her nose lifted in haughtiness. "Now leave me alone. I see that you have been drinking again. I have plenty of more important chores to worry about". So saying, she slammed the door shut.

The captain stormed back into his study. Pedro was still standing there.

"My good man what chores are you busy with, at this moment?"

"I was going to drop Ana back to the village".

"Would you be kind enough to do me a favour? Please take the carriage and escort the young lady from the docks. Offer her our apologies. Take Ana with you, if that's okay".

"Of course, master, consider it done".

Pedro was very dedicated to the Abranches family for whom his mother had worked, for many years. Pedro had looked after Captain Lino when he was a child and had taught him to love the land as he did. He was a great trekker and loved to spend time in the hills. His family lived close to the Abranches estate and after his marriage, he had moved into the estate as the caretaker of the Abranches holdings. This was a fitting reward for all the hard work he had put in, towards developing the property and fields at Oddavel village. In fact, it was he who had ingeniously developed the canal irrigation system on the estate.

As Pedro walked over to the shelter where the carriage was kept, his dear wife Ana sauntered over to him and hugged him from behind. "I thought you were going to drop me home on your bicycle but it looks like you are going to give me a ride home in the master's carriage!"

"You couldn't be far wrong. Hop in!" He said to his amazed wife.

Pedro had met Ana at the church feast in Pangim, a charming town close to Goa. Theirs was a love marriage and though her family had raised objections, she just wouldn't give up. They had lost their first baby due to a miscarriage. After a difficult pregnancy, a daughter was born to them. Sadly, at the age of 18, she had died in a tragic accident when she slipped into a pond full of reeds and water lilies, whilst trying to help some little boys retrieve a puppy from the water. The soft clay and the network of roots had made it difficult to save herself. This tragedy had devastated Ana who thereafter became frail and sickly. It was only through Ana's deep faith in God and Pedro's love for her that they had come to terms with their great loss.

...҈✦҈...

"I see a carriage approaching us", said the General, peering through shaded eyes at a fast approaching carriage. "This must be them", he said.

As the horses pulled up in front of the Viceroy's carriage, Pedro stepped down from the driver's seat and introduced himself to the General. "Good morning, Sir. I am Pedro Fernandes from the Abranches estate. I have come to receive Dona Paula".

"*Bom Dia*. So you have finally arrived. The lady has been worried that her employers have forgotten her totally", said the general. "But how do I know that Captain Abranches has sent you here?"

At that moment, Ana stepped out of the carriage, dressed in '*todop baz*', the traditional costume of native Goans. Before she could explain, Lieutenant Mariano interrupted saying, "I know Pedro very well. He has served the Abranches for many years".

"Come Senhora, your transport has arrived at last", said the General, opening the carriage door and helping Paula in. After doing the same for Ana, he leaned inside the window and planted a gentle kiss on Paula's cheek and bade her farewell.

"Thank you sir, for taking good care of me during the long and treacherous journey", said Paula with a grateful smile.

"I was indeed honoured to have a young lady like you who is a brave as she is pretty" he said.

Paula blushed at the compliment and said, "Thank you, Sir, and I wish you "*Bom Voyage*" on your journey to Macau"

As the carriage departed, Paula waved to Lieutenant Mariano. During the long wait, she had managed to say a quick farewell to Captain Joao.

Now turning to Ana at her side, Paula greeted her, "Sorry, we could not introduce ourselves properly. I am Paula".

"Pleased to meet you, Paula. I am Ana", and pointing to Pedro in the driver's seat she said, "He is Pedro, my husband".

"The Captain and his wife have sent you their apologies that they could not be here in person to receive you", said Pedro.

"That's okay", she said, "At last, I could meet *Avozinha* Catherine's nephew", she said, beaming at Pedro.

"How is Catherine?" asked Pedro.

"Oh, she is fine. She sends you her love".

"Welcome to Goa, my child. Don't worry. You are in good hands. We will always be there for you", answered Pedro.

"I know", Paula whispered warmly.

They had already passed under the Arch of the Viceroy and past the *Se Cathedral* and *Bom Jesus Basilica* and were heading straight to Ribandar. Soon they reached the *Ribandar* causeway, which was built by the Count of Linhares, the then Viceroy of Goa, across a swamp. It was completed in 1633. Before this, one had to travel to Pangim from the *Cidade* by sea!

The little town of Pangim was located on the banks of the Mandovi River. Like most typical Goan towns, it was built around a church facing a square. As they passed through a quaint neighbourhood with its shady cobbled streets, the picturesque red—tiled houses with decorative wrought iron balconies, brought back memories of the Portugal Paula had left behind. The old quarters, quaint homes, taverns and cafes made her feel she was truly in *Bairro Alto* in Lisbon. At the southern end of the neighbourhood, stood a pristine whitewashed chapel of its patron, St. Sebastian.

Pedro stopped the carriage at Pangim's main landmark, the baroque styled church of Our Lady of the Immaculate Conception which was built in 1541. It was planted at the top of the hillock with a series of zigzagging rock stairways leading up to it. It was bordered by rows of slender palm trees. An enormous bell hung from its central gable, centered between two stunted towers. This magnificent church was the first edifice raised by the Portuguese outside the walls of the city.

Pedro explained that this church was built for weary mariners to offer prayers of thanksgiving for their safe voyage to Goa. Travelling through the main thoroughfare *Avenida Dom Joao Castro*, they passed the Vice-royal lodge, a converted summer palace of the Adil Shah of Bijapur. A few kilometers down the road, they came upon a Church, which served the parishes of Santa Cruz and Taleigao villages. It had five altars and was dedicated to Our Lady of Safe Port, particularly dear to sailors and voyagers of the time.

"Look, Pedro, there is a horseman approaching us", said Ana, "I think it is the master!" she exclaimed.

"You are right Ana, it is the master himself!"

The rider pulled up in front of the carriage and dismounted with the ease of a master horseman. Pedro helped Paula out of the carriage again.

The tall and handsome young gentleman standing in front of her took Paula aback. She had imagined the Captain to be an elderly man, but he was surprisingly young.

"*Ola Senhora*, I am Lino", he said with a cheerful smile, "Welcome to Goa. My lady was not well and is resting. She is looking forward to receiving you at home".

"B . . . *Bom Dia Senhor*", said Paula, finding her voice at last. For some reason she could not look into his eyes. Pedro saw that the master himself was blushing and felt his discomfort.

"Pedro, take good care of our guest. She must be exhausted from the long voyage". Then, loosening a bunch of coconuts from his saddle he said, "Please open these tender coconuts and let Paula refresh herself". Lino swiftly mounted his horse and was off again.

"The Captain is a good man. A warm host", said Paula.

"Yes, my master is a good man", said Pedro proudly. But Pedro quickly changed the topic to his Aunt Catherine as he was longing to hear more about his dear aunt. "How is *Tia* Catherine? Does she think of Goa sometimes?"

Paula smiled at his query, "Frankly speaking, I never asked her that question. But I feel that she is torn between two loves—love for the Menezes family and love for Goa! Someday, she will want to come back to Goa for sure!" As she said this, her own situation was going to be like that of Catherine's and for a moment she frowned at the predicament. Pedro seemed to have read her mind, "My child, I know what you are thinking! You feel you are heading for the same situation, aren't you?"

Paula was amazed at the elderly man's astuteness. "You are perfectly right! How did you guess that?"

"Enough Pedro, let Paula enjoy her drink", Ana admonished her husband.

Soon they were on the road again, this time riding through the village market place which the locals called '*Tinto*'. Paula watched the natives going about their business of selling their fish and homegrown vegetables.

Suddenly Paula blurted out, "I love Goa oh so much!"

She had voiced her thoughts aloud and was embarrassed by her sudden interjection!

"You are just like your father!" commented Pedro, surprised at his own exclamation.

"My fa . . . fa . . . ther? Di . . . id you know him?" she asked, her eyes lighting up at once.

"Of course, I did. Didn't *Tia* Catherine ever tell you that?" he asked, surprised at her reaction.

"No . . . *Avozinha* never told me anything of that sort!"

"Well, whenever your father's ship came to Goa, he used to spend a day with us. We would take him to our village and spend time trekking through the hills and fields and fish in the village streams", he told her excitedly. "His heart was very much . . . wait a second, now you are your father's daughter . . . you have already seen this place through his eyes and through those of Catherine's . . . . That is why you feel so connected to this place!" he added.

"Yes indeed! My father's land of dreams, this is!"

"Now that you are actually in Goa, how do you feel?"

"I'm truly living in a dream", was the quick response.

...≫✦≪...

Soon the carriage arrived a tall wrought iron gate built into a high laterite stonewall. The Portuguese architects and builders were quick to recognize the quality and durability of this soft stone and many local masons were making their livelihood by quarrying and shaping them, even before the arrival of the Portuguese. The natives said the stone got harder with the passing of each monsoon season.

"Here we are at last! The Abranches estate", exclaimed Pedro, wiping the sweat off his brow. As they rode through the gates and onto the cobblestone pathway lined with exotic trees and flowering plants, the aristocratic manor dating from 1585, suddenly came into view. It had been built at a time when Goa was at its peak. It stood on a 2 acre plot and was designed by the same architect that had conceived the *Se Cathedral*".

Paula gathered her skirt and slowly climbed the twenty steps that took her to the covered portico at the entrance. The flooring was decorated with porcelain mosaic patterns, just like the ones seen in Portugal. The great arched windows had shell platelets in the timber shutters. She paused at the entrance, marveling at the family altar which carried the picture of the Sacred Heart of Jesus and Mary. Paula automatically made the Sign of the Cross. Pedro and Ana entered the great big foyer just as she did.

Suddenly, the silence of the huge house was shattered by a shrill voice, "Bring her up to my parlour, Pedro". Paula, who was startled for a moment, soon regained her composure.

"That is the mistress", said Ana. Paula said a silent prayer that God would grant her the patience and love to discharge her duties well, as she ascended the wide steps to the upper storey with Pedro.

The buxom Herodiana was reclining on an easy chair with both her feet on a leather upholstered Ottoman. She made no move to adjust her loose garment to hide her half naked breasts as she leaned forward to pick a fruit from a bowl of guavas and mangoes. Amidst the sweet scent of the fruits, Paula could distinctly smell alcohol in the air.

"My dear girl! Welcome to my household. You indeed look sweet", she declared, appearing very jovial. She got to her feet clumsily and embraced the surprised girl.

"You can go now", she said in a haughty tone, as she hugged Paula. At first, Paula thought that she was being addressed but Lady Herodiana was only dismissing Pedro.

"Not you dear. You are here to be my companion for the rest of your life. That tone is only for the pesky natives of this land", she said, the sweetness in her voice returning again, if only for a short while as she muttered under her breath. "I wonder how Lino tolerates that village bumpkin".

Paula was hurt by the comment but she quickly concealed her emotions under a smile, "I am glad to be associated with your household, Dona Herodiana", she told the lady.

Asking her to sit beside her, Herodiana called out to a maid in an arrogant voice, "Maria, get some refreshments for my new companion here", she said aloud, smiling at Paula.

Herodiana was of medium height, a little taller than Paula. Her figure showed traces of her past beauty. She was a little wide at the hips, but apart from that, she was sexually very appealing.

"Well Paula, tell me, how qualified are you?"

"I have studied ancient literature and History and I can speak fluent English", she confessed.

"*Tao bella*!" she exclaimed, but the joy was far from the truth as she hated anyone who was more educated than her. In fact, Herodiana had completed only her basic schooling followed by tutoring at home.

At that moment Maria, the maid returned, carrying a plate of crisp, fried breadfruit slices along with a glass of lemonade. It was now midmorning and a long time since she had the cool tender coconut water. Maria acknowledged Paula's smile of thanks and immediately introduced herself, "I am Maria. Welcome to Goa. If you need anything, please call me".

Herodiana had a scowl on her face. She hated any of her native staff to be friendly with any of her friends. "Go and prepare Madam's room and then come back to escort her there", she ordered, dismissing the maid as arrogantly as she had sent Pedro off!

"Paula, I have very simple rules in my household. Respect my privacy and be prompt to answer my calls. Remember, you are my lady-in-waiting that means you have to wait till I call you", she said laughing at the play on words.

Paula nervously nodded her head in acknowledgement.

"Also, do not be too friendly with the native workers here. They cannot be trusted. That is all. Now I shall rest. You may go and refresh yourself and join us for lunch later", she said, breaking wind unabashedly and excusing herself.

Maria stood outside the door stifling her laughter, waiting to take Paula to her quarters.

Paula liked her room instantly. The single wide window opened onto the Zuari River at a point where it widened its mouth to empty into the Arabian Sea. After having taken in a few fresh breaths of the cool sea breeze, she slowly pondered over why her room was situated so far from Herodiana's room.

The dining hall was elaborately laid out with carved furniture and gold-lined crockery and silver cutlery fit for a king. Paula wondered if all meal times were like this at the Abranches household. Her thoughts were answered when, to her surprise Herodiana entered the dining hall with Captain Joao and another guest, dressed in a black suit and clerical collar.

"*Ola Paula.* How do you find the Captain's *palaçio*?" he asked.

"Fabulous", Paula replied.

"And your hosts?"

But before she could answer that question, Lino entered the room and greeted everyone with a smile.

"Oh, hello Joao", he said, turning to the Captain and then turning to the Padre, "How nice to see you too, *Padre* Ivo"

"*Padre* Ivo is our good neighbour. You will be seeing him often at our place", said Herodiana, introducing him to Paula. For some reason, Paula did not like *Padre* Ivo at first sight. Was it because she had already caught him looking at her lasciviously? She hesitatingly offered her wrist to be kissed but pulled it away earlier than was expected. Herodiana noticed the bad chemistry and frowned. She did not approve of this behaviour, especially not with her friends.

Obviously, Ivo felt snubbed and gave her an icy look. Paula at once felt that she had gained an enemy in him. But it did not bother her. His sharp protruding eyes only went on to accentuate the cruelty that was hiding behind them.

"How was the journey, Captain? I heard you were attacked by pirates?" asked Lino, addressing Joao.

"Strange pirates these were! Not like the ones we usually encounter", he explained. "They were even flying a strange standard instead of the usual skull and bones!" It appeared that they were only interested in knowing if we had slaves on board. Once they came to know we were not carrying any, they just broke off, taking their wounded with them!"

"Sounds like our friend Captain Sergio and the French terror, Algernon. Our navy has been warned of their existence around the Mozambique Channel. They are badly affecting the slave trade and the King of Portugal has put a bounty on their heads".

Joao then looked at Paula and said, "Paula displayed great courage and humanity during the attack". He then went on to tell the gathering of how Paula had fearlessly defended a badly injured pirate. "Wow! That was commendable indeed", said Lino. But Herodiana was quick to show disapproval. "Paula, I hope you don't befriend my enemies", she said laughing at her silly joke, while Padre Ivo gave Paula a hard look.

Miguel Couto had acquired his new identity by a strange turn of fortune. Actually, he was a man wanted for murder in Macau. With the police chasing him, he had no other option but to hide in a thick forest. One day, whilst he was out hunting for food, he came upon a Jesuit missionary who was badly mauled and bleeding. His two other Jesuit colleagues had not survived the animal attack. Although Miguel wanted to remain undercover, he could not let a priest die this way. In his childhood days back in Portugal, Miguel had been saved from drowning by a member of a religious order. He gave up his cover and ran to the priest, offering his broad shoulder for support. What was amazing was the strange likeness they shared! Except for their hairstyles, both had a thin moustache and a sharp peaked nose.

"You are bleeding! We must get you to the hospital and fast! Who did this to you?"

"We . . . were attacked by bears . . . whilst returning from the village. Our guide . . . and two other colleagues were killed but . . . I escaped; I do not think I . . . will survive too long. Brother . . . I do not know if you are happy in life, but . . . if you are not and are seeking true peace; I . . . implore you to carry on my mission of love. The Chinese people . . . need to know Christ", he said this hesitatingly, gasping with great pain. With every word he spoke he was spewing blood from his mouth. It wasn't long before he breathed his last.

Miguel was thrilled at the God sent opportunity. The priest had just afforded him a chance to escape from his executioners. Quickly stripping the dead priest of his cassock, he donned it and without wasting time in giving him a decent burial, picked up the priest's bag which contained another two cassocks, a cross and some papers and made off in the direction of the city. Later, as he read the papers, Miguel was overjoyed! It was an order from Portugal, asking Padre Ivo to take up duties in the Santa Casa in Goa, as an Inquisition official. It was dated a month earlier. The good priest had not liked the idea of torturing people to be coerced into keeping the faith. Taking two other novices who shared the same views with him, he had taken recourse to the jungles of Macau, doing missionary service to the tribals who lived deep in the jungle.

But for Miguel, it was a golden opportunity to escape the law and live in luxury. He was aware of how the Inquisition officials lived in Goa which, he had heard was a land of opportunities. No sooner did he find a ship bound for Goa, Padre Ivo alias Miguel, reserved his passage, leaving behind all the insecurities of his gory past.

In Goa, no one dared to question him as he carried the order from the Pope himself. He took up residence in a place not far from the Abranches household in Oddavel. He was quick to make his acquaintance with Captain Lino and his eccentric wife and craftily gained their respect and trust, such that he was welcome to visit them any time he wished.

The Dona Paula Hillock
Photo by Soumyajit Choudhury

The Viceroy's Arch
Photo by Soumyajit Choudhury

Chapter 3

PRAÇA DE LEITAO
(The pig square)

————————— ❧ ❧ —————————

H erodiana kept many friends and she discriminated greatly even among them. The *Reinois* were women who came from Portugal as wives of officials and *Castiças* were those born to Portuguese parents in Goa; these friends were treated with high respect. The *Mistiças* who were women born out of mixed marriages between Portuguese men and African or native women, were held in lower esteem. The mix between Portuguese and African women were called '*mulattos*' and between Portuguese and natives, '*naturais*'.

Herodiana appeared to be totally devoid of creative pursuits unlike Paula who was a budding artist, poet and writer. However, she and her lady friends did enjoy one sport and that was horse riding. Most evenings were spent riding along the Mandovi River, dressed in fine apparels of velvet, damask, brocade and satin adorned with pearls and precious stones. Paula often would wonder if her lady was trying to impress someone. The pampered lady often left the house late in the evening when the Captain was away, wearing sweet smelling herbs and perfumes. If she did have a lover, it was a very well-kept secret!

Paula actually found her job very boring. Sometimes she had to accompany Herodiana to her friends' houses where she had to sit listening to her gossip and getting drunk on wine. Other times, she had to spend time at home, listening to her pompous tales. However, as days passed, Paula learnt to make better use of her time. Whilst her lady sat chatting with her friends, Paula wrote poetry and sketched the countryside and quaint, old houses. Also, every evening before going to bed, she spent some time writing the highlights of the day in her diary.

One day Paula was surprised when Herodiana asked her to accompany her to the market. Usually, Herodiana never went to the market herself. She had the local merchants bring cloth and jewels right unto her doorstep. Little did Paula know that what they were going to buy was far from cloth and jewellery. Pedro had prepared the carriage for the ride to *Rua Direita*. This street had a slave market called Praça de Leitao, which gathered once a week on Fridays. What was truly amazing was that the market was located right outside the Se Cathedral. It was obvious that even the church had accepted slavery as being an indispensable part of life!

Pedro carefully guided the horse drawn carriage through throngs of people of all kinds, crossing the street to enter the market. Alighting at the entrance to the Praça de Leitao, Herodiana and Paula slowly made their way towards the platforms displaying the poor human beings.

At first, Paula had thought that they were going to buy a horse since, during those days, Goa had gained a reputation of being an important distribution point for Arab horses. Fine Arabian studs were very much in demand in India and the Portuguese merchants found their trade very lucrative. Paula had often heard her father mention about this, as he was a great lover of horses. Paula had soon realized that she was wrong and that the Portuguese had another profitable trade going on with another form of livestock—human beings!

As they approached the slave market, at least five '*pombeiros*' approached them, taking their pith hats off in greeting. Each had slaves from India, Africa, Ceylon, Burma, Persia, Armenia, Malaysia, China, Indonesia and Japan. The '*escravas*' were female slaves. Black *escravas* from Africa were irresistible and were in great demand for their beauty. The Indian slave women with long black hair and big dark eyes were also very beautiful. The *pombeiros* used to get their slaves from the interiors of Africa; chiefly from Mozambique, Angola and Congo. Goa had predominantly black slaves but some Bengalees, Malabarees, Persians and Chinese were also seen. The aristocratic women used slaves to carry their palanquins. Even organizations like the *Misericordia* employed slaves. *Santa Monica* had 100 slaves, and an average '*casçado*' (Portuguese married to a native), had 10 slaves.

Being brought up in a devout Catholic family, Paula was not prepared for all this. She turned her eyes away from the nude slaves who were being herded like cattle. As she walked besides Herodiana, who was unmoved from all this, she prayed that one day this cruel trade would be banned by the King.

As they walked the stalls, the dealers called out the qualities, strengths, skills, etc. of the slaves on display. Herodiana had decided to bid for an African *escrava* and was meticulously noting down important information about a few slave girls.

"Paula, why are you standing so far away? Come here and help me decide which of this livestock to buy", asserted Herodiana, in a commanding tone.

Poor Paula was now forced to look up at the nude girls in front of her. As she cast her sad eyes from body to body, something around the neck of an African slave caught her eye. It was a simple necklace made of seashells but the type of shells and the arrangement on the string was very familiar. Herodiana was also attracted to the same escrava, but not for her necklace. She was truly a special slave. Her black skin gleamed in the sun highlighting her small but firm, peaked breasts. She had a glorious figure that most men would drool over. Her doe-eyes drooping with sadness, pouting lips and high cheekbones; all made her even more marketable. Herodiana smiled slyly as she looked at the slave. She imagined her dear husband Lino lusting for her. As long as Lino did not get in the way of her sexual pursuits she was okay with him going after the slave. During those days, it was not uncommon to keep female slaves to satisfy the lust of their masters and other male members of the household to which they were sold.

Many women of aristocratic backgrounds preferred to keep female slaves for their sons, rather than risk them going to the prostitutes. Besides, it was a cheaper option since prostitutes from Malacca were extremely in demand and also very expensive. They sat in palanquins borne by four male slaves with thighs and legs bared and extended, reclining on velvet cushions!

Often, slaves had to take the blame of their master's or mistress' follies on themselves as they carried on with their sexual excesses, while their spouses were away. For this, the slaves were later well rewarded.

Meanwhile, Paula's heart was pounding with excitement. She was now absolutely sure that the necklace was Clara's. She had to ask the slave girl where she had found it, hoping that she could lead her to where Clara was. Was she alive? How was she? Where was she? . . . . A million questions crowded her mind. Herodiana's shout rudely brought her back to the present, "Are you with me?" she screamed.

Paula felt embarrassed among the dealers "Yes, ma'm", was all she could say sheepishly.

"*Quanta custa*?" asked Herodiana to the dealer who owned the black escrava.

"She is expensive, *Senhora*. You can see that she stands out from all the slaves in the market. 50 *pardaos* and no less!"

Herodiana was very good at her bargaining skills and did not agree, "Look at her legs, they appear to have scales of a fish and her toes are curled and twisted out of shape. I will offer 35 pardaos and nothing more. Take it or leave it".

"40 *Senhora*, only for you".

35 *pardaos* and we have a deal".

"She is yours", said the pombeiro and made the slave step down from the platform.

Soon Pedro, Herodiana and Paula were headed back to the Abranches mansion with the dealer's horse-drawn cart with the escrava seated in it. Only this time she was clothed in a simple cotton dress. Paula looked at her and waved. The slave girl at first hesitated, not believing the kindly gesture from the lady in front of her carriage but later slowly raised her hand, waved back and smiled timidly.

...❧◆❧...

Paula could not contain her curiosity and excitement over Preta's necklace. This name had been kept for her by Herodiana because of her skin colour.

"Could it really be Clara's?" She wondered.

Paula had to find out right away and she had waited the whole day for night to come. As soon as the whole household was asleep, she tiptoed down to the kitchen, to the small storeroom where Preta was given a small corner to place her mat. As soon as she entered the room, Preta sat up with a start. She had been wide awake.

"Shhhh . . .", whispered Paula". It's me Paula", she revealed.

"*Senhora* . . . me do something for Senhora?" She asked fearfully.

"Please Preta, tell me where you got that necklace of yours. I just need to know it now!" Paula interjected.

With whatever Portuguese Preta had learnt from the market, she tried to get her message across to Paula". White lady in village . . . found in sea . . . Comoros . . . my friend . . . she give", She said.

"Can you tell me more about her dear?", pleaded Paula.

"She now go island . . . Madagascar . . . white man there", said Preta.

Although Paula guessed that Preta was implying that Clara was sent to the Pirate colony for some reason she felt that it was far safer there for Clara than with the black natives of the Comoros who did not speak her language nor shared her culture. That was all that Paula needed to know. She embraced Preta and cried out, "Clara is alive! Clara is alive! I must let Linda know as soon as possible!"

There were some trips outside the manor which Herodiana took by herself. On such days, Paula spent time chatting with the servants in the house. She loved their simplicity and humble nature. Soon she found that the natives of this land were very hospitable and could love as well as hate with equal emotion. Once you found favour with them, the relationship meant everything to them. Everyone loved Paula very much and appreciated her humility and sincerity. She never made the staff feel they were servants and heard them out and interacted with them at their level.

Gradually, Paula started accepting the invitations of staff to visit their villages and their humble abodes even though Herodiana had forbidden her to do so. She had grown very close to Pedro and Ana and spent a lot of time with them. Pedro took her around the village and all the beautiful spots only a local could know. One such spot was the rocky outcrop which rose straight up from a wooded area in Oddavel that fell sharply towards the sea. From this escarpment, one could watch the most beautiful sunset. For this reason, Paula had named the place 'Sunset Point'. She often stood at the edge of the precipice and looked at the horizon and wished that somewhere out there, Clara would be in safe hands.

"Magnificent! Truly amazing", she had exclaimed when Pedro had taken her there, for the first time. One Sunday morning, Captain Lino came home unannounced from one of his training exercises. Not finding Herodiana in her room, he decided to go up to the hill nearby. He loved to spend time outdoors in the woods and never wasted an opportunity to do so. On his way out, he passed Paula's room and wondered if she was back from Sunday service. He found himself blushing when he thought of her angelic face. He wondered what she did on her day off.

"What is happening to me?" he muttered to himself, blood rushing to his ears. But he couldn't help but admire her pleasant personality and the way she conducted herself. She was indeed special. He had even enjoyed overhearing her conversation with the native staff once, when he had visited the pantry to find something to eat and had lingered there, just enjoying the sound of her voice.

Captain Lino was a simple man, who loved the people who worked for him. Unknown to Herodiana, he often ate at Pedro's place. On an impulse, he decided to ride out to Oddavel knowing that Pedro would be home. So he mounted his horse and rode towards the sleepy little village. However, enroute, he changed his mind and decided to go to his favourite spot on the hill. So he tethered his horse to a tree and decided to climb on foot. On the way up, he stopped to admire the cashew apples which were almost ripe for plucking. He loved to drink 'feni', the intoxicating drink popular among the locals. The cashew nut, which grew outside the fruit, was a delicacy too. The locals roasted these on an open fire till the shells were black, and cracked the shell to extract the white edible nut from inside. As he bent down to collect cashew nuts from the foot of the tree that the crows had discarded after pecking away at the fruit, he suddenly heard a voice coming from the bushes nearby. He tiptoed to where the voice came from and there, near one of the trees overlooking the valley below, he saw an easel. He looked for the artist but saw no one. As he peered over the thick brush, he could see someone sitting with her back resting against the tree trunk, writing something. His heartbeat was racing now as he realized that it was Paula! Every now and then, she read out what she had written, before proceeding to write more.

"Hello", he called out softly.

Without raising her head from the paper, she said, "Jaku! I was wondering where you were today".

Lino's heart sank. Was Paula seeing someone? Was it why she was here? But the next moment he was chuckling to himself as he remembered that Jaku was the young son of his maid Maria. He usually looked after the goats from his farm! When Paula did not hear a response, she froze. When Paula turned to see who it was, she was so nervous that she dropped the ink bottle to the ground.

"S . . . Sir . . . ! I a . . . am . . . so . . . so . . . sorry", she stammered, as she hurriedly got to her feet.

"Relax, Paula, it's okay", replied Lino and sat opposite her, a short distance away.

"What are you writing?" he asked gently.

"I am writing a poem. This land is brimming with poetry . . .".

"Writing poetry? You remind me of my mother . . ."

"Was she a poet too?" asked Paula excitedly. Lino noticed the sparkle in her deep blue eyes.

"Yes, Paula. Infact, we used to carry her up to this very spot", he told her. "This is my favourite spot too. I am sure Pedro showed it to you".

"Yes, Sir, you are right. When he learned that I wrote poetry and loved to paint, he showed me this spot. It was he who escorted me up here and soon he will be back to take me to his house for lunch.

"I will show you my mother's poems when we go back to the house. Soon after I got married to Dona Herodiana, my mother suddenly took ill and passed away".

He had a blank look on his face. He was lost in his own thoughts. His mother's death was still a mystery to him. Until the first year of his marriage, she had been fine and full of life. However, Herodiana and his mother could hardly see eye to eye on anything. He remembered that fateful day when Pedro had burst into his office to tell him of his mother's passing.

"I wish I had met your mother", she said sighing.

Tears formed in his eyes as he thought of that terrible day. His mother had meant the world to him.

"I'm so sorry", said Paula, noticing the sadness on the Lino's face.

"No, no . . . don't feel sorry. In fact I am happy that you remind me of my mother. At last, I will have someone who can admire her poetry. Then, reaching for her writing pad, he said "May I?"

Paula blushed, "It isn't yet complete, sir"

Lino read the poem aloud,

"O Land of surf and sunshine divine

Gone are the days I wished you were mine

I hear your birds and smell the hay

I've eaten the fruit of thy soil

And grains borne from thy childrens' toil"

He paused suddenly as he recited her poem and exclaimed in delight, "How romantic! You are indeed a budding poet, Paula!" He was so touched by the poem that he leaned over to hug Paula, but at the last minute he drew himself back. Embarrassed by this sudden reaction, he quickly handed back the pad and hurriedly took her leave.

"Sorry, Paula, I have to attend to some urgent work this afternoon". He literally ran down the hill, with Paula staring after him with a bemused expression.

Later, Paula realized that she was to tell Lino about Clara and request him to do something to bring her back from Madagascar. Now the matter had to wait.

Back in the room that evening, Paula had begun to write letters to her mother and Helena all about her trip to Goa, the fight midsea, Clara, the Abranches household and all the wonderful people God had provided her to keep her from growing homesick. But she made very little progress as she could not help but dream of the Captain. She was surprised that she could actually sit and talk to him without feeling even a bit shy. There was something calming about his personality. But then, she brushed off such thoughts as being idle, as her mind commanded her to stay clear of married men!

After saying her prayers, she felt for the crucifix under her pillow. Instead of the cross, she felt something hard. It was a small box woven out of bamboo veneer. It contained a beautiful hand-woven woollen shawl with a large "P" embroidered at its two ends. Also, under the pillow was a book of poems, written in a scrawly hand and a note that said, "To our friendship".

Chapter 4

THE MARATHA ATTACK

Herodiana had known of Captain Lino's mission in the north of Goa however, she had miscalculated the time of his departure that day and had invited Amorous Bufon too early. There was no way of calling their meeting off since Amorous was already on his way. She had to think of something quickly to avoid getting caught with him. She nervously groped inside her chest of drawers for the pouch containing '*datura*'. Promiscuous wives used it to drug their husbands into a slumber so that they could indulge in their sexual fantasies with their lovers. Sometimes, husbands overdosed their cheating wives transporting them into permanent oblivion!

The captain was amazed at seeing Herodiana bringing him tea herself. Although he found it very odd, he decided to give her the benefit of the doubt and decided to have it right there on the bed, as she laid her head on his hip, stroking him erotically through the bed sheet. Poor Lino gulped the tea down quickly and placed the cup on the side-table hurriedly, drawing his wife towards him. It was a long time since he had received such treatment from his wife and he did not want to let go of the moment. But to Herodiana, every caress, every kiss was like torture and she pushed him off her in disgust as soon as the drug had taken effect!

Captain Lino served in the Portuguese army that largely consisted of native soldiers. The higher ranks were unquestionably held by the Portuguese. Everyone in the cavalry adored him for his honesty, bravery and loyalty.

The north-east territory of Sattari—the land of *'Sattar-vadi'* (seventy villages) was occupied by the Ranes, who claimed descent from the Rajputs of Rajputana. Sattari, a hilly and forested territory at the foot of the Western Ghats had proved to be a very fertile settlement with rivers and streams that criss-crossed its mountainous landscape of teak, eucalyptus and ebony trees, with grassy plains that served as pasturelands for grazing of cattle and goats. The Ranes and the Bhonsales from neighbouring Sawantwadi were constantly locking horns with each other over the question of the payment of feudal dues. To protect their rights and privileges, the kshatriyas *of Rajputana* were ever-ready to take up arms whenever their existence was threatened.

The Portuguese did well to capitalize on the disputes between the Ranes and their overlords and wooed them into becoming their allies in their fight against the Marathas and the Bhonsales. This alliance with the Ranes was very fruitful for the Portuguese.

The naval power of the Portuguese was strong and their ships would always cruise the coast to protect their trading vessels and thwart attacks from the ships of the Moors and pirates. Each fleet had a Captain under whose command were supply ships and barges larger than galleons, armed with artillery and well trained gunners. Since neighbouring Hindu kingdoms occupied Goan lands of Ponda, Pernem, Sattari and Bicholim, whose rulers were the Bhonsales, the Portuguese had to be ever vigilant against sudden attacks by them. About 200 soldiers guarded the Mandovi River from about seven bastions.

The Chapora fort commanded the hilltop at the north end of the bay. It was an exquisite and interesting fort built out of red laterite, which served as a border watch. It was complete with tunnels providing escape routes to besieged defenders if the need ever arose. The fort stood 22 kms away from 'Pangim'. The Aguada fort was situated at the mouth of the Mandovi River, 19 kms from Pangim. It was built around the same time as the Chapora fort and had a lighthouse with a room for storage of ammunition, a barrack and a church. Portuguese ships stopped there to take water from the seven springs which were part of the fort surrounds. The name Aguada came from *'Agua'*, which meant water.

Another fort that was an extention of the Aguada fort was the fort of *Reis Magos*, which got its name from the Church of the Magi kings in its vicinity. It was built around the same time and stood 6 kms from Pangim.

Although the attacks by sea were almost nil, land attacks however continued. Frustrated by their frequent raids, the Portuguese High command in Goa had decided to go on the offensive. Captain Lino Abranches was an automatic choice for one such attack on Ponda. After a successful early morning raid on the Bhonsales, Captain Lino was resting with his men on a wooded hill. That day, he pondered over all that was happening in his life.

"Herodiana . . . what a different woman she turned out to be after marriage . . . I never knew she would reject children".

By now, he had realized that his wife didn't love him at all. For years, his friends had been telling him to divorce Herodiana because they knew that she was cheating on him. But then, he had no proof and had resorted to drinking and other vices. He felt himself getting slowly attracted to Paula and this created an emotional crisis within him.

"I wonder what Paula must be doing right now", he said to himself, "she is so different from Herodiana . . . simple, caring and kind".

He had been happy about the evening just before he had left home. Herodiana had actually allowed him to make love to her. Although of course, he couldn't remember anything about it! However, even that joy was short-lived after he had discovered somebody's *'cravate'* inside the room. He wondered who it belonged to. He also pondered over some other things he had heard about Herodiana. For a long time, he didn't want to believe the tales, but now he felt that there could be some semblance of truth in them.

Suddenly, his thoughts were disturbed by a muffled rustling of leaves behind him. Instinctively, his hand went for his pistol and drew it out of its holster in a flash, covering the direction of the sound. But he relaxed when he saw that it was his second-in-command and close friend, Lieutenant Mariano.

"Thinking of Herodiana, Sir?" he said to the Captain.

"Cut that 'Sir' out! I told you that when we are alone and away from our men and the battlefield, we must address each other as friends", said Captain Lino.

"Okay . . . okay . . . but what is it that is troubling you now?"

"I was mulling over what you told me over dinner the other night".

"Well, that was what I overheard from others at the Recolhimento".

Recolhimento de Santa Maria Magdalena was a house for destitute women who had given up their evil way of life. Such women were called *'arrependida convertidas'*. This house was located near the Jesuit College of St. Paula at *'Rua das Convertidas'*. The house also kept women whose husbands were out at war or at sea.

"I know I believe all of you now. Just a day before we left on this campaign, I met that same doctor who revealed some horrific things about Herodiana", acknowledged the Captain, his mind racing to the visit.

Mariano did not interrupt him, as the Captain paused for a brief moment of silence and then continued remorsefully", I went to the *Recolhimento*, where I had kept Herodiana for three months before I went on a campaign. The person in charge there confirmed that my wife had been pregnant. According to him, just before I came back, she had left the house for a few days and had come back sick. Thereafter, there was no sign of the baby", continued the Captain, "Perhaps, after this campaign, we can go and see that doctor again".

"Sure amigo, I will accompany you if you wish", Mariano offered, "For now, we will concentrate on this battle".

"Just one more foray into the Bhonsales' base and then we can go back", the captain decided.

But fate had other designs. His friend Mariano was badly injured in an ambush by the enemy, which caught them unawares. Lieutenant Mariano had escaped with his life. Captain Lino fought like a lion that day and managed to make the enemy retreat. Keeping enough men under the charge of his trusted sergeant Andre, he rushed back to the city with Mariano.

After having placed Lieutenant Mariano in the care of the army hospital in Pangim, Captain Lino filed his report at the headquarters and rode directly to the city to meet the doctor.

"Ah, Captain Lino", the doctor greeted him cheerfully, "So, what was it, a boy or a girl??" he asked Captain Lino when he told him who he was.

"I don't have children and my wife cannot bear children!" he retorted.

"But when she came to me, she had been two months pregnant and very healthy too!" said the doctor surprised at what he had just heard. Captain Lino then told the doctor about how Herodiana had told him of her inability to bear children due to sickness

"That's not true, Captain, she is very capable of having children", he told him, "Since you have confided your problems to me, let me reveal something to you. Your lady was pregnant soon after your marriage and had come to me. But just like this time, there was no sign of her once I had confirmed the pregnancy".

"Is there anything else that you can tell me, Doctor?" pleaded the Captain.

"Well, Captain, the last time I met her, she was asking me to abort the baby. But I told her that abortion was a crime", said Doctor Fernando.

Dr. Fernando's last statement came as a bombshell to the Captain. It left him speechless. The only one he confided in was Mariano. But poor Mariano was fighting infection in his battered leg and if he did not respond well with the medicines, he could even loose his leg! He just couldn't get himself to go home. Then suddenly, he remembered that it was Sunday which meant Paula would be up on the cliff in Oddavel, where she usually spent her day off. Although he was unsure whether he could open his heart to Paula on this matter, he felt he had nobody else to talk to besides her. In any case, his marriage was almost over. By Catholic law, he could easily walk away from Herodiana since it would be proved that she didn't want to bear children and that she had had two abortions.

Captain Lino furiously rode towards the hill, hoping that Paula would be there. But when he reached the top, there was no one there!

"Maybe I am too early. I will wait" he thought. He sat against a tree trunk and fell off to sleep. When he eventually woke up, his heart skipped a beat. For there, sitting a few meters away was Paula, busy sketching. Like a true woodsman, he remained absolutely still, observing Paula fondly through his barely open eyelids. And then he saw Paula looking at him with loving eyes.

Suddenly he sat up, giving Paula a start.

"Sir, you have finally awoken!" She exclaimed.

"Please call me Lino when you are alone with me", he told her noting that she was blushing.

"You look so tired s . . . s . . . sir Lino . . . Lino" she said, correcting herself quickly.

"My best friend Mariano was badly wounded in the campaign", he said, with tears in his eyes, "And I thought of coming here to spend some time alone".

"If you wish . . . I will leave", she replied gently.

"No, no, no . . . . Please stay. In fact, it would be better to spend time chatting with you than wallowing in my sorrow", he replied quickly.

"So are you enjoying your stay with us? I hope you and Dona Herodiana are getting along fine by now?"

"Yes, I am enjoying every bit of Goa and the people are wonderful too. Madam is good to me too", she lied.

"You are truly a daring young lady to have travelled here all by yourself! Tell me Paula . . . . what is your ultimate dream in life?"

"To find the man of my dreams and have children of my own", she replied instantly. "What about you? Don't you love children?"

"Well it is a long story and more like a complex puzzle, the pieces are beginning to fit together now. Dona Herodiana has lied to me all these years that she could not bear children due to some sickness but I discovered today through Dr. Fernando that she has been aborting my babies ! . . . Sorry Paula . . . I did not mean to . . .".

"It's alright. If it helps to get it off your chest, please keep talking. I will not say a word to anyone about it", Paula promised.

"I've always wanted to have children and now to know that I could have had two, is tearing me apart. What a criminal!"

Paula was filled with pity for the Captain. Actually, she was bursting to tell him about all that was going on in the house behind his back but she knew that this was not the time. She had to wait for the right time to reveal all these things to the captain. After what she had just heard, any feelings of guilt of having been attracted to him had gone away. She had a strong urge to hug and console him. But she controlled her impulse. One thing could lead to another and before long, Dona Herodiana would come to hear of her affinity for the Captain and give her the excuse that she needed, to shame him in society.

Chapter 5

CAUGHT IN THE ACT

As soon as Herodiana doped Lino, she requested Pedro to take Paula on a sight-seeing tour of the City of Goa. She even gave Maria a day off in order to remove all obstacles from her diabolic plan. So far, all her plans for the day were falling into place. Only Preta remained and of course, her beloved husband Lino. But she had taken care of him too. Preta, as did the slaves from those days knew her limits exactly. It wasn't Preta that was bothering Herodiana at all. Actually, all preparations were made for her lover, who was nowhere in sight. She was furious with him over the delay.

"That Amorous doesn't know the meaning of time. Curse him", she said muttering, "Must be between legs somewhere . . . . wait till he arrives here!" Then she heard the sound of the main gate opening and ran back to the balcony.

"There he is, crazy man", she muttered again and then went to her room and shouted out to Preta "Go and get the gentleman in!" So saying, she went back into the room but kept the door of her room wide open. She was smiling mischievously as she crept under the sheets next to her doped husband. Her heart beat in anxious merriment as the heavy footsteps drew closer.

Amorous Bufon was a well built man with a barrel of a chest, muscles bulging from his tight shirt. He was only a little shorter than Captain Lino.

He was whistling a merry tune, as he drew near the door. Suddenly, he was rooted to the spot. His expression changed to that of someone who had just seen a ghost as he saw Herodiana lying next to her husband in bed!

As Amorous turned to leave, he heard Herodiana's peals of laughter, "Come back my love! He is well and truly drugged!"

...❧♦❧...

"Amorous, very soon you will have a widow to console", she said to him, after their violent session of love-making.

For a moment, her lover was confused with her words but then he understood and started laughing.

"Oh, poor Lino, I can imagine him lying on some lonely mountain, eyes wide open, staring blankly at the sky with a Maratha spear protruding out of his chest", she said, drawing a morbid picture of his rival.

His macabre laughter filled the room, interspersed with Herodiana's own squeals of delight as Amorous started caressing her body again.

"A spear of death for him, a spear of life for me!" she gasped in erotic pleasure.

...❧◆❦...

As Pedro and Paula made their way towards the Ribandar hill, Paula's mind was transported back to the day on the cliff. After their meeting on the hill, Paula had observed that the Captain was ignoring her on purpose. She hadn't yet thanked him for the shawl and the book of his mother's poems. She had even tried to make excuses to loiter outside his study in the hope of bumping into him. But there was no sign of him.

"Why is he avoiding me?" she wondered, her heart beating rapidly, merging with the clatter of the fast moving hooves of the horses. "We are fortunate to be away from the mistress today. She was in a foul mood. She even slapped Maria", interrupted Pedro just as Paula was slipping into an overwhelming melancholy.

"That wasn't nice", said Paula, forcing herself into a conversation with Pedro.

"What is that?" asked Paula, pointing to the two immense towers, rising tall above the treetops of the Holy Hill.

"That is the sixty-five year old St. Augustine's Church built by Augustinian monks who came to Goa some eighty years ago", explained Pedro. "On Holy Hill, you will see other important religious buildings too. The three storied convent and church of St. Monica was completed just forty years ago and is the largest convent in the orient. It was destroyed by fire thirty years ago and was rebuilt soon after", he continued.

Pedro drew up the carriage at the Church of our Lady of the Rosary, on top of the Ribandar hill. From there, one could get a breathtaking view of the entire Mandovi River. From here on, Pedro took Paula past a series of other noteworthy religious edifices like the Bom Jesus Basilica, with the Sé Cathedral opposite it, which was sanctioned by Viceroy Redondo a century ago.

"The southern tower of the cathedral has a golden bell made in Cuncolim in South Goa. It gets its name from its rich sound. It is rung at 5.30 am, 12.30 p.m. and 6.30 p.m. During the Inquisition, it is rung to announce the beginning of an *auto-da-fé*, which is usually held in the square in front.

"What is *auto-da-fé*?" asked Paula.

Pointing southwest of the Cathedral, Pedro explained, "The *'Oddlem Ghor'* as locals refer to it, is the Palace of the Inquisition. Blasphemers of the faith and heretics are tried there and later burnt at the stake in a ceremony that is known as *auto-da-fé* ".

Talking of the Inquisition was making her uncomfortable so she quickly changes the subject. "When I was on the ship, the Captain had explained something about the sacred and incorrupt body of St. Francis Xavier. Can we please visit his tomb please?"

"Of course, I will take you there. Ever since his mortal remains have been brought here, there is not a single man, woman or child who leaves the city of Goa without visiting the Bom Jesus Basilica. The body was brought to this Church fifty years ago".

"My father always talked about the great saint", said Paula". He told me that St. Francis Xavier is also called 'Apostle of India' and was born of noble parents in Spain. He arrived in Goa in 1542 and is said to have converted over 30,000 people to Christianity, established churches, raised the dead and healed the sick by touching them with his Rosary".

Pedro added, "I have been told that he travelled to Ceylon, China, Japan, and Malacca".

"Yes, while travelling to China, he got dysentery and died on the Island of Sancian. Even though his grave was filled with lime, the body remained in perfect condition. Later, his body was again removed and brought here on . . . here it is on this plaque . . . . March 16, 1554. He was canonized in 1622 by Pope Gregory XV and his body was then placed in this chapel of the Basilica of Bom Jesus", said Paula feeling pleased, that she remembered the story exactly how it was told by her father.

Paula was very quiet for the rest of the sightseeing trip, reflecting on the wonderful story again. She was tired and wished to return home. She wasn't yet accustomed to the humidity and heat of the place.

As soon as she reached the gate of the estate, Paula jumped out of the carriage and sped to the house hoping that her mistress was not upset with the delay in returning. The slave girl Preta was sitting at the foot of the steps. Preta had begun to like Paula very much as her humanity had touched her deeply. She was an angel compared to Dona Herodiana!

Now seeing Paula rushing towards the house, Preta blocked her passage and tried to explain, "Senhora . . ."

Paula was hardly listening, "Preta, please get me some water", she requested.

Preta gesticulated wildly, trying to dissuade Paula from going upstairs but as soon as she turned to go to the kitchen, Paula decided to check if Herodiana was awake. As she approached her mistress' door, she found it ajar and in the dim light of a candle, she observed a shocking scene! The Captain lay in deep slumber whilst a young and well-built man was making wild and passionate love to Dona Herodiana, who was totally ecstatic. Paula covered her mouth in total disbelief!

As soon as she gathered her composure, she turned around sharply and in the process, tipped a large porcelain vase to the floor. Not waiting to pick up the pieces, Paula ran down the stairs past a puzzled Preta holding out a glass of water and out into the garden, gasping for air. Paula had been too shocked for words and had blindly run out of the house as if a mad dog was chasing her. Her mind was a muddle of incoherent thoughts and feelings.

Out in the balcony, Herodiana stood half naked watching in dismay, Paula running out of the front gate.

"Merde! Wait till I'm done with you, Paula . . . you will regret this moment", screamed Herodiana, gesticulating wildly after her.

On one hand, Paula's mind screamed to return to Portugal. How could she carry on serving a nymphomaniac like this? On the other hand, how could she leave all the wonderful new friends she had made in Pedro, Ana, Maria and Preta? Also, she had grown fiercely loyal to the Captain and somehow felt that he needed her to be around, although of late, he did not speak much to her.

Hopping onto a bullock-cart that was carrying hay and dried cow dung to the village, Paula rested her head on the wooden side-rail, cushioned by her arm and closed her tear-filled eyes. The cart-driver, sensing that something may have gone wrong at the *'fidalgos'* house, did not say a word. Even when inquisitive passers-by made quizzical glances at him, he chose not to provide an explanation and kept on whipping his two lively oxen to step up the pace.

"Oh, how could she do such a thing to the poor Captain?" Thought Paula, with tears in her eyes.

Paula tried to make some sense out of all that she had seen, but there were no answers. "Was the Captain alive?"

If he was, he seemed to be totally oblivious of the heinous activity taking place right under his very nose!" It was all so very confusing for poor Paula. Was there something that Pedro and Ana were hiding from her? Could it be possible that Herodiana and Lino were having marital differences? She couldn't wait to reach Pedro's house and clear those things with them.

As they neared the village '*tinto*' or market place, she was suddenly jolted back to the present by the curious, prying looks of the villagers who seemed to be amused to see a 'firangi' lady sitting on a bullock cart.

Quickly snapping back to the present, Paula alighted from the bullock cart and thanking the driver, offered to pay for his services. But the driver refused to take any money, amazed at the thought of the white lady sitting on hay, inhaling the putrid smell of cow dung! But then, instantly he was filled with much respect for the young woman who had exuded much warmth and a sense of equality by lowering herself to their level. She was definitely unlike any of the other distinguished Portuguese women he had met before.

Pedro was surprised to see Paula at their doorstep. It wasn't long since he had escorted her back to the house after their sight-seeing trip.

"Paula! What are you doing here? And alone?" he asked with concern.

Ana, who was in the kitchen, came out to see who had come to their house. Seeing Paula, she immediately ran to her and gave her a warm hug.

Paula had a change of mind. As she walked up the red mud track that led up to Pedro's house, she had decided that she would say nothing about what she'd seen in the house. Not even to the Captain. She had decided that she would need time to mull over her course of action, because it truly was a sensitive issue. However, the immediate problem was to find an excuse for her being here! And she knew that Pedro and Ana would ask the inevitable question.

"You seem very disturbed. What happened? Can we help in any way?"

"Oh! It's nothing! I was disgusted with the way Dona Herodiana was treating Preta. I just needed to get away from the villa. I couldn't take the shouting and screaming. Poor Preta! Why did she have to be a slave? How I wish slavery was abolished!" she said.

"With the rate at which Goa is growing, we cannot expect slavery to be abolished at all! At least not for another hundred years", said Pedro, shaking his head from side to side, sighing.

Paula's mind wandered back to the attack on the *Santa Barbara* by the pirates near Madagascar. In retrospection, Paula quite liked the pirates after she came to know that their attack was with noble intentions of freeing the slaves and act as a major deterrent to this largely unfair human trade that was being propagated by the Portuguese.

"I know only one man who leads a war on slavery single handedly", said Paula, her eyes brightening up, "Captain Sergio".

"Sergio?" echoed Pedro, "But I thought he was a feared pirate?"

"Yes, a pirate he is, but a noble one at that! He frees slaves and houses them on his island. His community is notorious. The Portuguese government is wary of his raids on their ships and wants their band to be punished", said Paula sadly. "I wish there were a few more like Sergio", she added vehemently.

Ana, who was busy putting together a *'caldo'* in the kitchen before Paula had arrived, came in with steaming bowls of soup. It was dusk, and the dogs came out, expressing their authority over each other's territory and barking incessantly. The farmers were returning with their tired oxen from a hard day's work in the paddy fields, and the pigs were being called into their pens by their respective owners.

"Amazing how the locals use the pigs as scavengers to clear the human excreta from their toilets and at the same time, make sausages out of them! The concept of pig farming only for sausage making is totally unheard of in this part of the world", thought Paula with disgust.

"I am sorry I cannot give you a ride back in a decent carriage, but you can share the driver's seat with me. The cart, as you know, is for coconuts and is not fitted out with seats", offered Pedro apologetically.

"What if I told you that I got here on a bullock cart full of hay and dung?" Paula retorted with a smile.

Pedro was left speechless when he heard this. He just looked at her in amazement while Ana chuckled.

"That reminds me. I need to buy some dry dung—the chilly shrubs in my back yard need some manure. Pedro, will you arrange some from Shegun tomorrow?" said Ana. Dried cow dung served as a very good fertilizer for plants and fresh cow dung was used to coat the floors and walls of mud houses, to keep them cool and free from insects.

Later that evening, Pedro and Paula set out for the Abranches house. Paula's heart was pounding hard with nervousness, not knowing what awaited her.

...❦◆❦...

When she came back to the manor, she was shocked to see Preta crying as she opened the door. Her cheeks were swollen and her lips were badly bruised.

"What happened Preta?" asked Paula, with much concern. And, as the girl started to weep, she embraced her, understanding full well what may have happened.

"The lie I told to Pedro and Ana is indeed coming true! Me and my tongue!" Paula admonished herself.

"Please forgive me, Preta! I know it is my fault. I am sure she beat you because I went up to her room", cried Paula. Recognising Paula's voice in the entrance below, Herodiana called out to her.

"Paula, I have decided to send you back to Portugal. You have intruded on my privacy", she said in a firm voice. Paula remained calm. She bent her head and silently took all the abuses that followed. Once Herodiana was through with her barrage of words, Paula apologized meekly.

"Dona, I am truly sorry. I was only checking to see if you were cross with me for coming in late. I did not mean to spy on you".

"Spy on me! Spy on me? You inquisitive *puta* !" shouted Herodiana.

Swallowing the insults, Paula continued, "Forgive me *Senhora*, it was my fault. Please spare Preta. It is not her fault"

"Preta? Where is that brat now?" she shouted, stamping her feet in frenzy.

The frightened slave girl slowly showed herself. Herodiana pounced on her like a tigress, kicking her and squeezing her nipples till she howled in agony. Paula advanced forward.

"Don't you meddle in this Paula, or I will make little pieces of this African bitch and feed them to the dogs. Understand?" she yelled.

Tears rolled down Paula's cheeks and she fell on her knees and pleaded of Herodiana not to harm Preta. "Please stop. Punish me, not her!" She pleaded.

"Punish you? Wait till you get your due. I am not yet done with you!" She muttered venomously, and went back to her room, slamming the door shut behind her. "Get out! The two of you!" She screamed from inside, I don't want to see you again!"

Taking Preta by the arm, Paula led her to her room. "Don't worry, Preta. I will see what I can do for you. I must speak to the Captain. Of course, I will not tell him what happened today or else Senhora will kill you when he's away", she told the girl, giving her a big hug adding, "You can rest in my room if you are scared".

Preta started sobbing, "*Senhora*, no one has ever been so kind to me . . . ."

"Calm down, my girl, don't cry", Paula consoled her. "*Senhora*, you no fault . . . . Me told *Senhora* I broke vase . . . you come back to collect shawl", revealed Preta.

"Poor dear, why did you do that, Preta? Paula asked, tears rolling down her cheeks, at her brave attempt to cover for her.

"Ma'am . . . I just animal. I born this way. My mother die this way. No use life!" She said humbly.

"Shhhh . . . Don't speak that way, my girl. God loves you. He created everyone equally. One day you will have the freedom that you desire. You be a free person!" Paula declared solemnly.

Early the next day, Paula made her way up to the Captain's room, with a heavy heart. The room was adjoining Herodiana's and she was terrified that she could be discovered. She wanted to see him regarding Preta but as an excuse, she was carrying the book of his mother's poems. She also knew that Herodiana never awoke that early. Seeing the door slightly ajar, she knocked softly and slowly pushed it open.

"Excuse me, Sir, are you there?" she asked.

Except for the sound of the wind making clicking sounds as it played on the multiple Mother of Pearl platelets in the window pane, there was pin-drop silence. The desk was clean except for a quill and an inkpot. The heavy iron family seal and a bar of lac lay on the table. She hurriedly left the room and closed the door. At that very moment, Pedro who had come silently up the stairs, made her freeze in terror. "Relax, my child. Are you looking for the master?" he whispered.

"Ye . . . ye . . . yes", she stammered, "I wanted to return the journal of his mother's poems".

"Oh, the Captain left this morning. He had urgent summons from headquarters", he told her.

"But the door was open", she said, pointing to the door.

"Oh that! The Master never locks his room". He revealed with a smile. "He has always been a trusting person. Sometimes . . . too trusting!" He murmured. "Do you know when he will be back?" enquired Paula.

"No, my child, he told me that he would return soon. I think he is fighting the Maratha insurgency somewhere on the borders of Portuguese-Goa".

That morning, Lino had awoken feeling very groggy. He was surprised to see Herodiana, sleeping in his room next to him. She was fully naked and the sheets were crumpled. "Had I made such wild love to my lady after almost a year?" he mused. But he had been confused because he could not remember a thing. "Maybe I was too drunk to remember", he thought.

"I am sure that Dona Herodiana wanted me to make love to her badly. After all, we have not been intimate for quite sometime now. She must be having a change of heart towards me after all", he thought. Although he had felt aroused looking at his nude wife next to him, he decided against giving vent to his cravings and instead, planted a kiss on her cheek. Soon after that, he dashed off to his headquarters.

...❧♦❧...

When Paula returned to her room that morning, she knelt down, joined her hands and prayed, "Please Lord, keep the Captain safe from all harm and bring him back unhurt". Then, she reached for her journal under her pillow and felt something else there! Preta had left a gift for her; her shell necklace. Paula had forgotten all about Clara. Suddenly she felt a rush of guilt feelings coming over her. She blamed herself for not discussing the issue with Lino.

"I must visit Linda today and tell her all about Clara!" she decided.

...❧♦❧...

The morning following that fateful night of the attack, when Clara was thrown overboard and had found the makeshift raft and floated on it, the fishermen from the Comoros Island were returning to their shores, pleased with their abundant catch of lobster and shrimp. Their fishing boats were fairly small, being about twenty feet in length, rowed by four to five men. The early morning sun had just appeared in the east however, the thick fog was making it difficult for them to navigate the rocky shores safely, so they waited for the fog to clear. As usual, they called out to each other making familiar clicking sounds with their mouths. As each boat responded to the call, a cacophony of quivering tones could be heard through the mist.

Meanwhile, the bundle on the raft stirred and slowly blinked and opened her eyes. It took a while for her damp body to return to its senses. For a moment, Clara did not know where she was. All she could see was the raft and nothing else. She pinched herself to convince herself that she was alive. And then, the weird voices confused her even more. "Where am I?" she wondered. Soon the memory of the frightful night came rushing back to her. She was alive and they were human voices that she was hearing! Clara tried to shout for help but weak as she was, only a hoarse whisper escaped her lips. She had to attract the attention of these strange people speaking in a language she had never heard before. If she was not found and fast, it was sure death for her. The cold and hunger had already diminished her will to stay alive. There was only one way she could attract their attention and that was to make a loud noise. After giving up on trying hard to dislodge a plank from her makeshift raft, she could resort to only one tactic—to plunge herself into the water, making a big noise. Reluctantly, Clara stood at the edge of the raft and let herself fall flat on her back into the ocean with a big splash.

The voices suddenly stopped to listen and then thinking that a colleague had fallen overboard, they came paddling towards the spot where the sound had come from. One of the men screamed with fright as Clara caught hold of his oar and touched his wrist.

There, in the slowly clearing mist and the soft glare of the early morning sunshine was a pale-faced, white woman, almost dying with fatigue and cold. The leader of the fishermen, decided to haul her into his canoe and cover her with his coarse wool blanket to keep her warm. The fishing party made for shore excitedly with their strange catch.

Meanwhile, at Madagascar . . .

Captain Sergio had been a little disappointed with the outcome of their attack on the Santa Barbara and its fleet. A ship of that size could easily have carried at least 200 to 300 slaves below its deck. Although there weren't too many casualties in the fight, there were many who were injured and were now convalescing in the warmth of their own beds in their cottages.

Looking over the cliff, towards the bay below, he could see his men mending the ripped timber on *Trovão's* side. Some of the other smaller ships had also suffered some damage. Even the sails were getting patched up with the help of the womenfolk stitching the pieces of fabric onto the holes. The storehouse was well stocked for emergencies like these, with cured timbers and sail fabrics.

Some of the carpenters were already taking a 'chai' break inside a lean-to shelter that was prepared on the beach to shade them from the hot tropical sun. The women had prepared a sweet dish from corn. Soon, the others also started approaching the shelter for their share of the refreshments.

The camaraderie amongst the men was commendable. Each one was like family and treated one another with love and respect. Even the women roamed freely without fear of getting abused. Disobedience to the code meant sure punishment. Some unfortunate ones had walked the plank with a heavy stone tied round their neck. Others who had disobeyed were banished from the island to the neighbouring kingdom of Mohili where they had to fight for the king against his enemies.

"What are you looking at?" Came a gruff voice from behind Sergio.

"Just spending time by myself. Enjoying the activity below", He replied calmly.

"If you continue like this, I am afraid that all the pretty women out there will die waiting for you!" He quipped.

"My type of woman has not yet been born in this world", he replied curtly.

"Maybe one of these days you will meet one, on the Portuguese ships we board", said Algernon.

"Speaking of which, I was told that there were some very young and good-looking ladies on the ship the other night! It appears that ladies have now started braving the seas to reach Portuguese colonies in the east"

"If nothing works, we will get you a nice native Madagascan! In fact, it would help us get a truce with them", joked Algernon.

The natives had grown wary of the foreigners occupying their island but they could not do much to get rid of them because they were mainly farmers and cattle-raisers. On more than one occasion, the natives had tried to scare them off the island with some grotesque masks.

As they looked out towards the bay, they spotted a small boat approaching the shore. It was surely not one of theirs, and some of the gang had already lined the beach to challenge them.

Sergio and Algernon decided to go down and see what was going on.

...❧✦❧...

The small boat was guided expertly onto the beach by the four strong Africans. Seated in the middle was a fair-skinned lady who was unmistakably an European. One of the men helped the lady get off the boat whilst the other emptied the boat of the fruits that the King of Mohili had sent to his benefactors.

The leader of the men spoke in a strange African tongue, "The great king of Mohili sends you his greetings. This white lady was found floating in the sea by our fishermen who brought her to the village. We do not know her language and the king thought it was better to hand her over to you"

When Algernon asked the lady her name in French, she answered in Portuguese, *"Eu sou Clara"*.

CHAPTER 6

COULD IT BE CLARA?

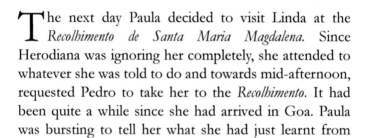

The next day Paula decided to visit Linda at the *Recolhimento de Santa Maria Magdalena.* Since Herodiana was ignoring her completely, she attended to whatever she was told to do and towards mid-afternoon, requested Pedro to take her to the *Recolhimento.* It had been quite a while since she had arrived in Goa. Paula was bursting to tell her what she had just learnt from Preta.

As soon as the carriage came to a halt at the foot of the long flight of steps leading up to the portico of the *Recolhimento,* Linda, who was chatting with a group of friends, seeing Paula, jumped out of her seat and ran down the steps joyously.

"My dear Paula! Welcome! So very good to see you", she exclaimed, embracing her warmly.

Whilst still in the embrace, Paula exclaimed, "Clara is alive! I think I have proof!" She held out the shell necklace to Linda.

Linda immediately recognized the necklace that Clara had worn on the ship. Overjoyed at this wonderful news, Linda knelt down on the hard pavement, forgetting the pain of the pebbles biting into her knees and praised God.

"Where did the necklace come from? Where is she now? Can we meet her . . . ?"

"Calm down Linda, I only know for sure that she is alive and well. The necklace was given to Preta, our slave girl from the Comoros islands. Clara had given the necklace to her as a token of her friendship and gratitude for nursing her back to health after she was found by fishermen, floating on a few planks of timber that had been ripped off from the ships during the encounter with the pirates.

Linda's face suddenly tensed at the mention of the pirates, but Paula explained, "Yes, she was found by the fishermen and then the king of the Comoros decided to hand her over to his white friends, the pirates from the island of Madagascar. But don't be too afraid of this since I have heard that these are a different brand of pirates altogether! They free slaves from their captors and then offer them freedom. It has been said that they have a big community on the island of Madagascar.

"If the pirates are such nice people, why then did they not arrange to send Clara back on the many Portuguese ships and other trading ships that ply those waters?" asked Linda earnestly.

Paula was silent for a moment, realizing what Linda was saying was true. The pirates could have sent her back to Goa easily if they wanted to.

"But what if Clara herself decided to stay back on their island? What if she found the people and surroundings favourable? Maybe over there it is better than life in the Recolhimento? Isn't that possible?"

It was Linda's turn to be quiet. So many 'what ifs' were running through her mind.

"Let's not worry about things we cannot control. Let us make a confession of faith that she is well and keep thanking the Lord for this! We will soon find her. Tell me about yourself Linda. How has it been with you?"

"My life was so boring all along until now. I feel I have found my true love. The dream of my life! He is so very adorable".

"Are you going to tell me about him or not", asked Paula impatiently, leading her to a wooden bench under a jackfruit tree in the garden.

"I have been volunteering as a trainee nurse at the army hospital in Pangim, since they are short of nurses. The recent scuffle with the Marathas has brought in many injured soldiers and one of them was a lieutenant . . . ."

"Mariano, Lieutenant Mariano!" shouted Paula, "Is that his name? Lino was on this mission and his second-in-command and best friend Lieutenant Mariano was badly wounded in the fight".

"Yes it is !" Linda exclaimed. "What a coincidence! I have fallen in love with the same person you speak of. Life is so wonderful! I had in fact locked eyes with him on the dock when we first arrived in Goa. I had taken an immediate liking to him then and now our paths have crossed again! We have decided to marry as soon as he is out of hospital!" she exclaimed.

"In fact, I was going to the army hospital to see him after meeting you. Would you like to come along?"

Linda was overjoyed however, she wanted Paula to request the *Regente's* permission to take her out. The *Regente* was a sweet elderly lady who at once obliged and soon they were on their way, chatting exuberantly while Pedro enjoyed his handmade cigar made of tobacco rolled into a dry jackfruit leaf!

The army hospital was a big building situated along the *Praia de Gaspar Dias* road. A wide canal carried the city's storm water from Altinho hill right down through the settlements of St. Inez and Miramar and into the Mandovi River. Several horse carriages, which were modified to serve as ambulances stood outside the hospital. As Linda led Paula to the room at the end of the corridor, Paula cringed at all the unfortunate injured men, many without legs or hands, anxiously awaiting their passage back to Portugal. The native soldiers had several visitors to see them in the hospital. It was a lonely life for the Portuguese soldiers in Goa, and that was why the Portuguese king was encouraging the *Orfaas del Rei* (Orphans of the King) to find Portuguese suitors in Goa.

As they entered Mariano's room, Paula now knew at last why the Captain was missing from home all these days. There he was, sitting at Mariano's bedside, chatting. Both of them were surprised to see the two ladies there. Linda wasted no time in hurrying to Mariano's bedside, carefully bent over him and planted a lingering kiss on his lips. Lino just held Paula's gaze speaking yet without saying a word, leaving only their enamoured eyes to do the talking.

Linda quickly chipped in excitedly, "And Paula will be my maid of honour".

For a moment, Lino tensed and Mariano at once felt his nervousness. Understanding fully well his quandary, he said, "Don't worry, my friend. The wedding won't be a big affair. Only the four of us will be present at the little cross at the Oddavel jetty".

Paula then embraced Linda with tears in her eyes. "I am so glad that you have ultimately found the love you were looking for!" Then looking at Mariano, "From what we shared of each other's lives onboard the ship, I can only say that you are a very fortunate man in taking Linda for your wife".

"And the same goes for Linda!" asserted the Captain, "Mariano is an honourable man and Linda will treasure his caring and cheerful company. Consider yourself fortunate to have such a man as your husband!"

Just as Linda was blushing, Pedro knocked at the door. Mariano called him in, but he merely popped his head in through the door and greeted everyone and said, "Sorry, Dona Paula, but we really must go if we are to reach the Recolhimento back in time".

"Oh thanks for reminding us Pedro, we will be out in a moment", said Paula graciously. "Come on Linda; let your man rest his eyes now!"

Lino could not take his eyes off Paula as she left the room with Linda. Mariano took notice of the gaze and shook his head from side to side, sighing loudly on purpose.

Chapter 7

KIDNAPPED!

Lady Herodiana was well and truly drunk when Padre Ivo visited her after the episode with Paula discovering her in bed with Bufon.

"*Puta*! I hate her! I hate her!" she kept on hissing in rage.

"What happened? Who has done this to you?" he asked.

"Paula! The whore! She knows of my relationship with Amorous", she screamed.

Padre Ivo knew all about Amorous Bufon and Herodiana's affair. In a fit of holy passion, and of course drunkenness, she had confessed all of their 'sins'. But instead of absolution and prescribing penance, Padre Ivo had laughed it all off! From that day on, Herodiana had begun to like him until, one day she had introduced Amorous to him! Padre Ivo and Amorous were like birds of a feather. Amorous was born out of wedlock, to a

Portuguese *'fidalgo'* who had an affair with one of his African slaves, a 'mulatto" maid. The good thing though was that he had acquired the complexion of his father. His mother had brought him up through hard work but when he was just twelve, he had beaten her up badly because she had refused to tell him who his father was. A week later, she took her life, out of sheer desperation. Young Amorous had to take to the streets and soon fell into bad company. He was arrested by the police, when he got involved in a dockyard brawl. At the age of nineteen, he had murdered the man who he learned was his father. He was caught and sentenced to spend time in a prison in Mozambique, a Portuguese colony. During his tenure there, he had befriended an African native and studied voodoo. They had both succeeded in escaping to Brazil as stowaways, after nine years of hard labour in prison. Both had lived in the forests of Brazil for four long years before finding a merchant ship bound for Macau where he befriended a young nobleman whose father was a blind count who lived in Goa. He had killed this nobleman and taken his identity.

At age 34, he had come to Goa, posing as Henri de Almeida, son of the eccentric blind Conde de Almeida. The poor old man, believed him to be his son and willed his property and title to him. He died as a result of a mysterious illness. The only other person in the house, who had known the real Henri, was also silenced two days after he had questioned Amorous Bufon. He was found dead at the foot of the tallest section of the mansion, probably pushed down from the tower.

Armed with a title, which also gave him a job as a military consultant to one of the Portuguese garrisons, stationed near Ponda, he flirted around with the beautiful women in the elite officers' club. At one of the parties, he had met the beautiful Amarella de Cabral, daughter of a rich military officer and had married her at the age of 36. However, he was not sexually content with the beautiful but frail Amarella, who he later discovered to be an epileptic. At this time, when their relations grew strained, Amorous met Herodiana at an army celebration and was beguiled by her beauty. Herodiana, who herself had taken a liking for him, reciprocated his approaches and soon got involved in a torrid, carnal, relationship. In her, the three most important things in life had been fulfilled, sex, wealth and a good social standing. Herodiana agreed to address him as Amorous Bufon and not Conde Henri, to keep his identity confidential.

Padre Ivo, Amorous and Herodiana had become great friends and more so, Ivo and Amorous. Together, they were responsible for settling old scores with Amorous' enemies. By that time, Padre Ivo had won repute as being a hardened Inquisition official. His methods of torture were known to be the cruelest. He had once had a man's ear cut off and fed to the same man after roasting it on a spit. One of Amorous's enemies, a Conde was conducting enquiries about him. Ivo and Amorous plotted against him and had him incarcerated for heresies. All this was made possible by Padre Ivo for the promise of prime property next to the river.

Today, they were sitting in the balcony of the same
mansion plotting to frame Paula and thereby create an
excuse to send her back to Portugal.

It was February and carnival time in Goa. The City
of Goa had put together a grand cultural event just
to impress the special emissary of the King who was
visiting Goa for the first time. Many of the noblemen
and their household were encouraged to participate in a
grand parade, dressed in fancy clothes, to march past the
Viceroy's palace.

Pedro told Paula about the parade but she was not too
keen on going all the way to the Viceroy's Palace to see it.
Also, Herodiana would have declined permission to do
so in any case! The idea of a parade brought back many
memories of Portugal and the lovely *'entrudo'* there. As
she sat in her room, thinking of home, she heard a knock
on the door. An excited Preta stood at the door, "Ma'am,
come, see, beautiful . . . music".

The slave girl took Paula to a balcony overlooking the
courtyard of the mansion. And from there, Paula could
see a beautiful sight, something that filled her heart with
joy. Dragging Preta by the wrist, she ran down the steps,
taking them two at a time with Preta almost flying behind
her. The man holding the reins of a pumpkin carriage
was dressed like a bee, sitting in the driver's seat which
was shaped like a flower. The driver was playing a lively
tune on his well-used violin. It was a masquerade!

As Paula and Preta drew close to the gate, the driver stopped playing and said to them,

"Hello ladies, put your hand into the back of the pumpkin and choose yourself a free gift".

"Stay here, Preta, let me get a gift for you", said Paula, opening the great big iron gate enough to slide herself through it. As she opened the doors of the pumpkin to reach inside, a strong pair of hands grabbed her from inside and she felt someone push her in, from the outside. Within a flash, the driver was back in his seat, whipping the horses into a frenzied pace.

At first Preta did not realize what was happening, but when she saw the carriage had taken off with her beloved Paula inside, the slave girl ran inside the house screaming hysterically.

By the time Pedro gave chase on his cycle, the carriage had already disappeared from sight. Pedro was close to tears as he returned home dejected. He wished that the master's horse was in the stable. All Pedro could do was to lodge a complaint with the police and wait for the master to return.

When Pedro went in to inform Herodiana about the kidnapping of her lady-in-waiting, she clutched her chest with one hand and with the other, covered her gasping mouth and sat heavily on a chair with a wild-eyed look on her face.

"Kidnapped?" was all she could say in feigned disbelief, then she buried her head in a velvet-covered cushion and made loud sobbing sounds.

Pedro did not know what to make of this reaction and left the room, closing the door softly behind him, "Could it be possible that Herodiana loved her?" he wondered.

As she slowly descended to the living room, he saw Preta, sobbing her heart out on one of steps of the stair. He brushed her hair gently and said to her, "We will see Paula again. The master will bring her back".

...❧ ♦ ❧...

Meanwhile, Lino had decided to return home from the army rest house where he was spending his days in silence, away from his broken home. He had quality time with himself and with his dear friend Mariano, who by God's grace was slowly recovering. However, the Captain knew that Mariano would not be declared fit for the army again. The doctors had to amputate his right leg upto the knee.

There were moments when Lino blamed himself, "Maybe I could have saved his leg had I to reach him to a hospital quicker", he lamented. He was missing from the manor for almost a week and although he loathed seeing his cheating wife again, something inside him warmed up to the memory of his dear Paula.

As Lino approached the ornate wrought iron gates that opened into his estate, he felt deeply happy for the first time as he steered his handsome Arabian steed through the entrance and into the garden leading up to the entrance of the manor. Maria who was in the garden burying used tea leaves at the base of the rose bushes as fertiliser, greeted him with a sad face and walked up to the stables to get Pedro. "Something's definitely wrong", he thought, "Maria had not given her usual full blown smile, exposing the gap in her front teeth. She had not rushed inside as she normally did to get Pedro. For the first time, he had seen sadness in the normally enthusiastic lady. A crestfallen Pedro greeted him 'Bom dia'.

"Is something wrong, Pedro?" he asked, suddenly feeling the tension in the air. "Is the mistress okay?"

Pedro was choking with emotion as he waited for his master to dismount. He hardly said a word of greeting as he led the horse to its stable, but Lino stopped him with a firm grip on his shoulder, "Tell me what happened".

"Paula has been kidnapped".

The words stung. "Kidnapped!" He exclaimed, "By whom?"

After a big pause, he said, "My dear man, tell me how it happened".

With tearful eyes, Pedro told his master all that had happened.

After hearing him out, Captain asked Pedro if he had lodged a complaint with the authorities in the City of

Goa.Seeing that Pedro had already done that he sent a message to his headquarters to find out whether there were any Maratha infiltrators in the colony.

Whilst all this was going on, Lino had completely forgotten to ask about his wife. Suddenly, he remembered her. He had come prepared for a face-off with her regarding the abortions but the news of Paula's disappearance had shattered his spirit. "Could Herodiana have had anything to do with this?" he wondered, getting up from his writing desk and pacing the timber floor of his study. But then Pedro had told him how she had reacted when he had told her of Paula's disappearance. "I cannot trust the lady. If she could fool me all these years, she can easily act shocked and hysterical", he thought.

On the way to Herodiana's room, Lino paused at Paula's door, angry at what had transpired. Red-faced, Lino went upstairs to confront his wife. As he opened the door of her room, he was taken aback to see her weeping. As soon as she saw him, she came running towards him and embraced him, sobbing bitterly on his broad shoulders.

Lino stood there, holding Herodiana loosely. At that moment he did not know what to make of her reaction and he stood there frozen in her embrace.

For two whole days, Lino arranged a posse of friends and looked for Paula everywhere. Short of entering the enemy camp, they left no place unearthed but to no avail.

Her captors had not left a single clue that would lead them to her.

"Oh Paula, where are you, my dearest?" he lamented silently. "I know that you are aware of my sufferings but yet you were so understanding not to interfere in my marriage".

Meanwhile, Herodiana had arranged with Bufon to secretly deliver her a food parcel which she had hidden in her room and did not suffer a bit from Paula's loss. She had acted so well that even the staff at the manor had begun to believe that their mistress was indeed affected greatly by Paula's disappearance. Hearing of her husband's grief and his refusal to eat anything, she was very jealous that another woman who she disliked was desirable to him. This made her unhappy. The only consolation she received was from the news that Amorous had given her. Lino had been ordered to leave for the island of Madagascar to annihilate the pirates who were troubling the Portuguese ships from there. All Herodiana hoped for was that her husband would not return from the campaign.

Chapter 8

THE TRIBUNAL OF FIRE

The froth-crested waves crashed on knife-edged rocks that jutted out into the sea. Little crabs were seen crawling back into the crags to escape the thunder of the waves. But each time, the waters receded to be one with the vastness of the sea after bathing the rocks with their saline spray. The wind, which was watching this wonderful drama, turned into a gentle breeze. It caressed with love, the green fronds of the tall, serpentine coconut palms, which seemed to touch the heavens. Traversing the golden sands of this glorious, sun-kissed land, a gem on the west coast of the Indian Peninsula, it continued inland, holding the laughter of children and sweet whispers of lovers in its breath. But, suddenly . . . there was a lull. The heart-rending cry of one in pain, shattered the tranquility of the dusk, and in the sky, the ball of orange suddenly seemed to have ducked quickly below the horizon in trepidation. Even the moon decided not to show its face that night.

The *'Santa Casa'* reverberated with the blood curdling screams of a man in agony. In the center of the Palace, below a massive dome decorated with frescoes depicting heaven and hell, was the biggest array of torture machines one could ever imagine. However, today there was only one unfortunate soul that was receiving the 'treatment'. Strung high atop a wooden gibbet and moaning in pain, was a man stripped completely of his clothes save his loincloth. His hands were tied in a strange fashion; forced backwards, folded at the elbows, with palms facing each other. The rope was tied around the wrists and threaded through a pulley at the top. The other end was wound around a wooden drum that was being turned by a burly operator. As he turned the drum, his sweaty, bulging muscles glistened in the flickering light of the candles on the walls. The man tied to the rope was being hoisted right to the very top of the gibbet. The drum was locked in position with a timber wedge, the operator waiting on orders from the hooded man, seated high on a throne-like gilded chair, placed on a beautifully carved timber dais.

"Francisco, confess and we will pardon you"

"Mercy, mercy, Padre . . . I beg you . . . spare me from this torture . . . I-I-I have done nothing wrong, I swear"

The Inquisitor turned to his aide who was sitting at his side on a lower chair and they both looked at each other and slowly shook their heads from side to side. At the thud of his iron staff on the timber deck, the operator of the gibbet released the wedge in one swift motion and let the drum unwind the rope, letting Francisco freefall at least twelve meters from underside the tall, cobwebbed soffit of the dome. The hall once again reverberated with piercing screams as the sudden stretch on the man's arms tore at every sinew in his body. And through the grating of several square openings in the floor, sighs and murmurs of pity could be heard of the prisoners from the dungeons below.

Strangely, Christ's eyes on the lifelike crucifix on the wall were wide open; as if watching in total disbelief, the Inquisitors who were striking terror in the hearts of the innocent victim of the torture.

The breeze, angered by this gross misuse of God's authority, turned around and blew angrily back towards the sea . . . a mighty wind of wrath!

The '*Santa Casa*' was situated next to the great square in front of the cathedral dedicated to St. Catherine. It was a majestic building with three arched front doors, the central one of which, led to a flight of steps which ascended to several rooms for the officers of the house. The two flanking doors led to the grandiose apartments of the two inquisitors, one of whom was called the '*Inquisitor Maior*' or chief inquisitor. These were grand enough to arouse the jealousy of even the Viceroy and the Archbishop. Situated deep inside the building was a gallery of about two hundred cells, each about ten square feet in area. The walls were about five feet thick. Each cell had two doors within this wall. The inner door had a pass-through hatch, from which the prisoners were served their daily ration of food. The outer door was of heavy iron construction. The cells had no windows. The dark corridor resounded with the sound of moans, sighs and the clinking of chains as the prisoners shifted uncomfortably in their cells.

Unlike other cells, the one at the end of the corridor, was occupied by a white woman of Portuguese birth. She had been brought in only a few days ago and hardly spoke a word to the other inmates during their evening walk in the guarded courtyard. It was being whispered that this white woman was found in a trance, in front of a stone deity, deep in the forests of Bicholim, further up north of Goa where the Hindus held fort. Some said that she had been drugged with '*Datura*'.

...⚜...

The next morning, her memory started unclouding, disconnected scenes flooded her mind and nothing was making sense to her. As she searched in vain for a reason for being held captive, the sliding of the heavy bolt of the outer door of her cell, raised her hopes of being released from this rude nightmare. But to her dismay, only the hatch door opened and an earthen bowl of fresh fruits, bread and sausages was passed to her.

The European prisoners were better treated. In the mornings, they received a loaf of fresh bread, fruits and sausages. On Sundays and sometimes on Thursdays, they received meat and bread, a dish of rice and curry. On weekdays, dinner consisted of fish, bread, rice, curry and eggs. The native prisoners were given only '*kanji*' (rice broth), rice and fish. The momentary opening of the hatch door revealed an earthen bowl for ablutions and an earthen jar for drinking water. In the corner stood a broom and on the side wall, a bench with a mat on it for sleeping. Folded neatly at the end of the bench was a quilt that only European prisoners were given, to be used as a mattress or as a cover against mosquitoes.

Francisco Mergulhao had been dumped into a fetid cell which was provided with a hole for relieving himself, but it overflowed, letting off an abominable smell. He was imprisoned unfairly because the lady he visited frequently was being eyed upon by a relative of the Governor of Damão. Damão also belonged to the Portuguese crown and came under the jurisdiction of the City of Goa for administrative purposes and therefore, the Inquisition and all its atrocities also applied to the people of Damão. Francisco had later learnt that the jealousy of the Governor's relative had won him a most feared rival. To make matters worse, a native priest associated with the Holy Office also nurtured a strong passion for the lady making a common cause with the Governor's relative. Both these rivals had joined forces to invoke ruin on Francisco, thus making the Inquisition, to order his arrest and incarceration.

The Inquisition was the greatest terror in Goa because of its incredible tyranny. It was a totally independent operation which did not recognize the Viceroys as their superiors. The words *'auto da fé'* reverberated throughout Goa and those accused of heresy, necromancy or blasphemy were tried and burnt at the stake during these *'auto da fé'*.

As soon as Francisco had recovered from a day of torture, he was dragged in for another dose of it.

"Mercy, mercy . . . Please . . . . I have done nothing wrong", screamed Francisco from atop the timber tower.

Once again, the heavy set man, the Inquisitor Maior nodded his head from side to side, "the qualifiers of the Holy Office have examined your case and have confirmed that you Francisco, have acted against the purity of the faith".

The lawyers assigned to Francisco had twisted his honest statements, giving the inquisitors false testimony. These lawyers were *'Familiares do Santo Officio'* and usually consisted of justice officers whose job was to accuse the prisoners. They were not paid salaries but carried out their duties with a false sense of honour. Many of them came from nobility and so received a gold medal with the inscription of the Holy Office.

As Francisco was dropped repeatedly from the top of the gibbet, his arm muscles strained with the sudden jerk of his bodyweight pulling down on his arms, sending agonizing pain shooting up through his shoulders. But the screams of agony fell on deaf ears.

"Confess your crimes against the Holy Church and we will consider your pleas for mercy", was all that he got from his inquisitors.

Francisco's screams mingled with those of others who were being punished in the same torture chamber. A woman stripped completely of her clothing was being forced to imbibe cup after cup of water. Her feet were tied together at the anklets and shackled to the floor. Her hands were tied to a rod across which she was made to arch backwards. Soon, the weight of the water became so great at one point that it made her choke as it gushed out of her open mouth, stifling her scream forever.

Another, a man named Agnelo Gomes, a new convert who had returned back to his old religion, was having the soles of his feet buttered with pork fat. He was then strung upon an iron chain and lowered towards a fire, link by link. He had been handed over to the Inquisition by his own brother for practicing what he swore to be, witchcraft. The inquisitors had confiscated his properties and auctioned these at the Rua Direita, the main thoroughfare in the City of Goa. They had already decided that he would die at the next *'auto da fé'*.

Back in solitary confinement, the young lady struggled to get her memory back. She couldn't even remember her own name. All she could remember vaguely was the huge black stone idol at whose feet she had been thrown. Her thoughts were rudely interrupted by piercing screams of agony which seemed to come from the other side of her wall. She put her ear hard against the wall and tried to listen. All she could hear was the voice of her neighbour, Francisco with whom she had chatted in low tones during their walk outside, just the day before.

"God, give me the strength to bear this persecution when my turn arrives", was all she could gasp out as her frail body trembled uncontrollably with fear.

It wasn't until the arrival of the jailor with her dinner that she unbundled herself from the hug she had given herself; her chin on her bent knees, arms wrapped around the shins, drawing them close to her bosom. Instead of the latch opening up to pass her food, the inner door was being opened. She was paralyzed with fear as an elderly jailor entered the cell with a candle. In the dim flickering light, she watched the jailor's jaw drop and release a gasp "Paula! Is it really you?" But there was no sign of recognition on the lady's face. "Lino has been looking high and low for you over these last few days. Oh my God, I have been asked to bring you to the 'Hall of Torments' my child and that, I must do or risk getting tortured myself", he cried. Paula showed no signs of recollection at the mention of the name as she trembled at the thought of what her torture would be.

For the moment, there was nothing he could do for Paula. He just walked her sadly to the now deserted hall. The torture machines were bloody and resting after a day's work of tearing limbs and scalding feet. Both the inquisitors had decided that they would treat themselves to some post-dinner entertainment. Paula was stripped naked and strapped to a ratchet. The jailor closed his eyes tightly and tried to look the other way. He was asked to turn the wheel that stretched her limbs very, very slowly. Paula twisted in agony with the stretch, as her tormentors transfixed their eyes on her exquisite figure and whispered lascivious compliments to each other. He tried to relax the stretch but the inquisitors urged him on. The unfortunate girl screamed in intolerable pain of her torture. Her mind was switching on and off. As the cruel men applauded her angelic face and the brightness of her eyes, Paula had begun seeing a thousand images projected by her agonized brain; Images from her childhood in Portugal and then in Goa. One of the inquisitors was commenting on the voluptuous contours of her breasts and the shape of her buttocks. The pain made the images turn around faster and faster and suddenly, she gasped out, "Help me Lino, my love help me, and so saying, she passed out.

Disappointed about the sudden end to their entertainment, the two officials left the large hall, leaving the jailor to attend to Paula, Seeing them leave the hall, the jailor hurried towards Paula to loosen her from ratchet. He carried her to her quarters and placed her on the bench. Covering her with the quilt, he went back to his quarters, a broken man. The past month had been terrible enough. He just could not bear to see the torture inflicted on the poor innocent prisoners of the Inquisition. When he had left the army, he had never imagined that his new job would be so heart-rending!

As a jailor, Andrew had occasionally been assigned to the ratchet. But those who were trussed to it were people unknown to him. Of all the people he had to torture,

Paula caused him the most guilt and hurt because he had seen the affection his previous master had for her.

His thoughts wandered back to his army days when he had killed many an enemy, fighting for the King. But he did not regret killing those men, since given the opportunity, they would have killed him too.

Andrew adored Captain Lino, who he knew to be a compassionate officer, loved by one and all under his command. Andrew had served as a sergeant to Lino then. In fact, he had known the Captain's family for a long time; since their families were neighbours back home in Portugal. But there was something much greater than just old associations that bonded him to the Captain. The infantryman turned jailor owed his life to him! A couple of years ago in an attack against a Maratha camp, the Captain and Andrew had been separated from the rest of the men. Faced with superior force, they had to retreat into the dense undergrowth. Andrew had fallen into a trap that was laid by the wily Marathas. He had fallen into a deep hole in the ground that had been covered by some dry sticks camouflaged with leaves. Lino had taken cover very close to where the hole was. Fortunately for Andrew, his moans had been heard by the Captain, who had silently crept towards the pit and peered in. Luckily for Andrew, he had fallen right between the spikes that were placed inside the pit. However, both his legs had been fractured.

As the Captain had contemplated what to do next, he had heard Marathi speaking soldiers scanning the bushes for them.

"Quiet, Andrew! Soldiers", he had whispered.

"Leave me and save yourself. Let me die . . ." but before Andrew had completed his plea, Lino had screamed loudly and had charged at the two Maratha soldiers with his sword. The shout had distracted the soldiers long enough for Lino to deal with one of the soldiers, finishing him off instantly with a decapitating blow to the head but the other, sidestepped his charge and brought his sword heavily down on the Captain. Lino tripped on a protruding root, just in time as the sword struck the root, slicing through it easily. Holding the blade of the sword, he had yanked it with all his might, bearing the pain of the sharp blade as it cut through his palm. As the soldier toppled over him, the Captain had held his own blade up, letting the body weight of the falling soldier do the rest.

Despite his bleeding hand, Lino had quickly cut a vine off a banyan tree and had managed to help Andrew out of the pit. Forgetting his own injury he had carried Andrew on his shoulders all the way to the base camp.

It was during Andrew's visits to the Captain's house after his recovery, that he had met Paula. A few weeks earlier, he had met a very distraught Captain Lino. He had been deeply affected by the kidnapping of Paula. In fact, he had even taken leave from his duties to help look for her. It was no secret from the Captain's state that he was indeed in love with her and he didn't blame him at all for that since he knew what a vile person Herodiana was.

"At last we have found Paula! How glad Captain Lino will be when I tell him", thought Andrew excitedly.

Soon after his duty, Andrew headed straight for the River Zuari, where Lino usually took his early morning walk. It was best that he avoided anyone seeing him with the Captain since Andrew was mortally afraid of being spotted by the many spies of the Inquisition.

Andrew watched the Captain tie his horse to a fence at the Oddavel side of the Zuari River. The sun had just begun to raise its lustrous face above the hilly plains, bathing the river with a soft and silvery sheen. The early morning dew was still in the air and on the leaves of the cashew trees that dotted the hill slopes, which led to the rocky laterite plateau above. With childlike exuberance, Lino stepped onto a black laterite rock that was projecting out into the river. Leaping from one rock to another, he was soon standing atop the furthermost rock into the river. And there facing the sun, he stood balancing on one leg with the other foot placed on the knee, hands clasped high above his head. It was a strange but beautiful posture which he held for quite a few minutes before he alternated his leg.

"The Captain is doing Yoga and Yoga is only practiced by the Hindus!" Andrew's brains screamed with fear for the Captain. He knew that such an act was foolhardy and that the Captain could get into serious trouble with the inquisition! Leaving his sheltered place, he ran to the rocks taking dangerously wide leaps, in a bid to get to the Captain quickly.

"*Mon Deus*! Don't do that!" he gasped as he reached the spot where the Captain stood. "You can get into serious trouble for that". Without disengaging himself from the pose, the Captain turned his head enough to look at Andrew and smile, "They cannot touch me. Besides, I hate them for what they do in the name of religion. I regret my non-action over my dear Hindu friend Laxman, who I respected very much as a good human being. But see what they did to him only because he was helping other Hindu converts to flee from the persecution".

Laxman was the village faith healer and lived a good and simple life with his wife but they caught him and branded him a 'sorcerer', and tortured and burnt him at the stake.

"I wish I had tried to save him. His death haunts me and if ever again, such a thing happens to someone dear to me, I will personally free him from the prison of the Inquisition and burn the monstrous place down!" He said with much remorse.

"Sir . . ." Andrew started to speak but stopped, fearing a horrific reaction from the Captain, " . . . I am here to tell you something that may warrant just that! It is about Paula!

"What about her?" shouted the Captain, his face growing taut with anxiety.

"Paula has been imprisoned at the *Santa Casa*", he whispered, choking with emotion.

The Captain almost fell off the rock, and had it not been for Andrew's quick reflexes, he would have fallen into the river. "*Disgraça*! Paula imprisoned? But for what?" he shouted in disgust.

"Someone has framed her and falsely accused her of blasphemy and idolatry. She was found in a trance-like state, prostrate before a Hindu deity in some forest in the north of Goa", explained Andrew.

"Is she well?"

"I am afraid to say that she is being tortured mercilessly and I have heard that she will be burnt at the stake for crimes against the faith. The '*Auto da Fé*' will take place at the '*Campo Santo Lazaro*'. I had no choice but to operate the torture instruments on her or I would be tortured myself!" sobbed Andrew.

The Captain had tears in his eyes as he patted Andrew on the back. "There is no time for that now! We need to work fast. But will you help me save her Andrew?" he asked pleadingly.

"Even if I have to die in the process!" exclaimed Andrew.

"I wish I had listened to you when you told me not to leave the army. There is no justice here. The life of the prisoner means nothing. All that they want is to confiscate land and wealth. Even the seven witnesses' word to confirm the crime, is connived", said Andrew regretfully.

"Forget it, my man. Let's hasten and make plans for her rescue", the Captain told him in a serious tone, his mind already in battle mode!

Chapter 9

THE 'AUTO DA FÉ'
(Act Of Faith)
───── ⌧ ⌦ ─────

F rancisco had learnt that the *Auto da Fé* would take place the following day. But he had not expected the noisy opening of the heavy steel inner door at 2 a.m. in the morning! He was ordered to wear a black robe with a white stripe running down the middle, front and back, and dragged to the gallery where almost two hundred victims were standing, reclining against the wall. There were both men as well as women, dressed similarly. Then big scapularies of yellow fabric with the cross of St. Andrew painted on the front and back were brought out, to be worn by some of the unfortunate who were lined up in the dark gallery. These scapularies were called *'sanbenitos'*. These were reserved for those converts condemned of having committed crimes against the Catholic Church, be it Jews, Muslims, magicians or heretics.

Those who were branded as convicts and persisted in denying the facts of which they were accused of, were obliged to wear another scapulary which was called *'samarra'*, a brown cloth on which the portrait of the victim was painted above flames with demons around it. Below the sinister drawing were written the names of the condemned and their crimes. But those who accused themselves, a different *'samarra'* was given. In these brown vests, the flames were facing downwards (called *'fogo revolto'* in Portuguese). About twenty of the *sanbenitos* were given a cardboard painted cup with demons painted over them with the word *'feitiçeiro'* written on it. These were persons who were accused of necromancy.

At 5.30 a.m, the sun slowly broke free from the line of hills that were hiding it, causing the birth of a fateful day for those unfortunate souls. The bells of the *Se Cathedral* were tolling; a signal for the people of Goa to wake up and witness the ceremony of the *'Auto da Fé'*, which was considered to be the triumph of the Holy Office.

Each of the condemned was ordered to march alongside a *'padrinho'* (godfather). It was considered a great honour to be appointed a godfather for these ceremonies. Francisco's godfather was an admiral of the Portuguese armada. Paula appeared very tired and worn after repeated summons for torture. She was fortunate that her torture had been less intense since the inquisitors wanted to ensure their entertainment each night. The inquisitors had reluctantly passed the death sentence on Paula, since their nocturnal pastime had become the talk of the *Santa Casa*. They had to let go, hoping that someone as good as Paula would come their way some day.

Andrew had told Paula, to continuously raise her hands and bless the people gathered there. This would be a sign for the Captain to identify her in the procession.

"Fear not, my child. Today somehow, your beloved master will save you", was all that he had uttered, with rock solid confidence in the Captain. By now, Paula's memory had been restored to her fully, perhaps by the pain from her torture!

The procession was taken through the long streets of the city, so that the multitudes could watch the ugly pageant. Finally, covered with shame and confusion, the condemned reached the Church of St. Francis, which was decked up with great pomp. The altar was covered with a black cloth on which stood silver candelabra. On both sides of the altar, there were two kinds of thrones; the right for the Inquisitor and his counselors and the left side for the Viceroy and his court. The convicts and the godfathers were seated on benches.

A hush fell on the crowd as four muscular men carried life-sized statues accompanied by four other men carrying an equal number of boxes full of bones of the victims who had died by torture. Their statues, clothed in *samaras* and representing the dead victims would be tried too. Once the long sermon concluded, two officials went up to the pulpit to read publicly the proceedings of all the guilty and to declare the sentence upon them. Francisco released a sigh of relief when he was declared ex-communicated. His belongings would be sent back to his home in Portugal and he would have to serve five years on the galleys in Portugal. He also had to comply with other penitences imposed by the inquisitors.

The condemned to be burnt at the stake were delivered to the secular arm of the church, to which the cruel inquisition begged to use clemency and mercy, and to impose the death penalty without the effusion of blood, which meant burning at the stake. Thus, Paula was led towards *Campo St.Lazaro* to be burnt alive.

Meanwhile, the disguised Lino waited beside a huge laterite boulder that was left uncut by the masons who were in the employ of the Inquisition to build platforms with stakes, since the number of condemned heretics was on the increase and the ceremony was taking too long to complete. Lino had been working throughout the night. He had managed to smuggle a few boxes of gunpowder from the ammunition store and had emptied them in the crevices of the huge boulder. The fuse was kept long enough, to allow him to time the explosion well. Years of experience at timing the canons to go off at set intervals, on Goa's many ramparts was soon going to pay off. The procession was nearing the place where Lino was hiding. He carefully scanned each unfortunate victim of the cruel Inquisition and for signs of Paula. After an excruciating wait, he saw her waving her arms from side to side, obviously tired of making the sign of the cross over the people. She had been doing it for quite some time now! As soon as Lino had identified her well, he set the fuse to go off exactly when the front portion of the procession would pass by the rock.

After what seemed like an eternity, the charge blew the rock into small fragments, raining the people with stones like hail from the skies. The deafening sound and the stinging stones made the procession break up as people ran helter-skelter for cover, expecting another blast. Before the second charge had even gone off, the captain had already run towards where Paula stood, rooted to her spot in shock, making it easy for Lino to spot her in the milieu. Lino hurriedly knocked off her head-dress of flowers and tore her scapulary from her body and whisked her off her feet, placing her over his muscular shoulders, and racing for the dense cover of the trees. Within minutes, they were galloping through the thick brush, deep into the forest.

Lino had surveyed the terrain well and had chosen an excellent spot as a hiding place. Deep in the forest there was an abandoned laterite stone quarry. Back in the days before the Portuguese had occupied Goa, Hindu masons and sculptors had worked there to prepare the stones to raise their magnificent temples. But the Portuguese had razed them to the ground, building in their exact location gigantic churches, flaunting renaissance and gothic architecture. The same masons and sculptors continued to work on the churches and unearthed all the good quality stone from the quarries that littered the countryside.

Lino guided his horse carefully down into the abandoned quarry until he came to a shelter carved out of the mountainside. The masons had used their break times well, carving into the side of the mountain a beautiful shelter, complete with rooms inside! Lino had already stocked the place well, with biscuits, fresh bread and fruit preserves. Lino had even taken care to bring her suitcase with her clothes. There was a spring nearby which provided ample water for drinking and bathing.

Paula had not uttered a word since the time they had arrived. She clung to Lino tightly, afraid of letting go, lest he disappeared from her sight. The torture and lack of sleep had taken its toll on Paula. Only their hearts spoke as neither wanted to break the silence nor the loving embrace. The Captain awoke the next morning to the realization that there was something warm cuddled against his hairy chest. Paula awoke to the light, lingering kiss that Lino hesitantly planted on her forehead.

"My saviour, my life from now on is all yours. I will not be able to live without you. I will kill myself if anything happened to you".

"Hush, my love, for now you must only think of getting your strength back as fast as possible. I cannot be with you for long. Neither can I leave you here all by yourself. I have to keep you somewhere safe until I can decide how to handle this situation".

The shelter prepared by the long-gone masons was a reasonably comfortable one. It was comparatively safe as hardly anyone ventured into that quarry. The superstitious natives avoided the place as they believed that it was haunted.

In the loving arms of her beloved, Paula slowly regained her strength. Now it was almost a week since she had been rescued. She had told Lino of her suspicions regarding Padre Ivo. For some reason she felt she must not tell the captain about Amorous and Herodiana, at least not just yet.

"I am quite sure that it was him in that pumpkin carriage that day", she told him.

"Forget that day dear, and all that followed it. Now you are safe and I will ensure that you are well protected from all your enemies. I know I cannot leave you alone here but I have a plan and tomorrow you will have a proper home for yourself, with two wonderful people who will dote on you. My leave ends tomorrow and i will be reporting to my headquarters tomorrow but I will soon be back with you", he told her, kissing her palm.

Panic was written all over her face and eyes. Paula did not want him to leave her even for a minute. However, she knew she could not have him with her for obvious reasons. He had to return home as if nothing had happened to him. He could not afford to arouse any suspicion. Lino's face melted when he looked at her sad face. He gently wiped away her tears and hugged her.

That afternoon, when Lino got up from his siesta, he saw Paula lying in his arms, kissing him gently and nibbling at his ears. This time, he could not restrain himself from kissing her full on the lips.

"*Meu Amor*, oh my darling . . .", she whispered and closed her eyes as he kissed her passionately. Very slowly, his hands reached under her blouse caressing her firm well formed breasts, feeling her nipples harden at his touch. Her nails dug into his chest with wild ecstasy as she yielded to his touch. He undressed her gently and allowed her to feverishly undress him. As he buried himself gently into her warm and gyrating body, she wrapped her legs around his waist, moaning joyously as he made love to her with a tenderness and compassion like he had never done before. As the two lovers climaxed in perfect unison, both experienced a heavenly kind of bliss.

Lino rolled over still keeping her wrapped around his body, caressing her supple and smooth buttocks. "Thank you, my love for loving me this way", she whispered running her tongue over his lips teasingly.

... ❧ ♦ ❧ ...

Greg McKenna was an elderly Irish doctor who lived in a village which was a few kilometers from the quarry. He had been living in Goa since the last twenty years, studying ancient medical practices of the natives. In fact, he had even married a local woman. Goa was well known for medicinal practices, which were prevalent before the advent of the Portuguese.

When his wife Sabita told him that a handsome Portuguese officer had dismounted at their gate, he was a little apprehensive. He wasn't expecting anybody.

"I wonder why an army man is here to see me", he remarked anxiously but soon relaxed when he saw who it was.

"*Madre de Deus*! Lino, It's you!" he exclaimed with genuine joy and ran down to the door to receive him.

After the cordial hugs and greetings, Lino introduced the rejuvenated Paula to the McKennas. Sabita led Paula by the hand into the verandah and sat there chatting. Meanwhile, Lino confided everything to Greg, trusting him completely to keep the secret.

"Lord! What great suffering she has gone through! The so called Holy Inquisition that you Portuguese started is so very unholy indeed!" he exclaimed in disgust. "Don't worry Lino, my boy", he said cheerily. "Paula can stay with us for as long as she likes".

The Se Cathedral
Photo by Soumyajit Choudhury

The Basilica of Bom Jesus
Photo by Soumyajit Choudhury

Chapter 10

PAULA FLEES

aula loved the McKennas very much. They were extremely loving people who showered a lot of care on her. Sabita was so much like her *Avozinha*, and had told her about Goa and its Hindu customs and many other interesting things about her peoples' culture with an intimate knowledge that Pedro and Catarina had lacked.

Parting from Lino had been very painful but by now she had known how to handle it. Besides, she had begun to enjoy the daily trips to the forest with the McKenna's. She used to sit with the other women of the village, while Greg went about his work with the natives who inhabited the woods.

As the days passed by, Paula became very worried. She started experiencing nausea and vomiting in the morning. At first she thought that it was from the exertion of household chores but it continued even when she was in the house doing nothing. She had already missed a monthly cycle and was approaching another. Moreover, she had every reason to suspect that she was pregnant. It appeared that the passionate night in the quarry had taken its toll.

Paula was petrified. If anyone discovered that she was pregnant, she would have to explain how it occurred. She didn't want to expose the good Captain, who she loved very much. She would do anything to save him from such a scandal. However, that 'anything' would not include telling a lie and blaming someone else for her condition nor could it include abortion!

"You can get rid of that child before it is born", said a persistent voice within her. But she had always been pro-life. Being a staunch Catholic also helped her nip the thought instantly.

"*Mae*! I need you now more than ever", she whispered sadly to the cool breeze from the nearby river which caressed her pale cheeks.

"I know what I will do. I will leave myself in the hands of my heavenly Mother", she said to herself as she remembered her mother's final words to her, "When I am not with you, do not forget your heavenly Mother who will always be there for you".

Paula hurriedly packed up her belongings. As she was throwing them into her suitcase, she found the shawl given to her by Lino.

"Oh my sweet lover, I wonder how you would take this news. How can I ever tell you that I will always love you. Surely, we will meet someday in another world and then you will know that everything I did was for your best", she said fighting back her tears. Ever since her romantic attachment to the Captain, Paula had been treasuring her shawl like it was a priceless heirloom. She lovingly kissed the shawl and wrapped it around her neck, picked up her suitcase and crept out into the night. She wore Greg's old pair of riding pants and his cap on her head.

It was a moonlit night but a strong gale was blowing from the nearby river. It was one of those nights which, though not very dark would make one stay inside. Paula was glad that she had thrown on the big, black jacket, the Captain had left behind. As Paula reached the river bank, she felt the fear in the pit of her stomach rising into her throat. She was very scared. Though she had been a tough young girl, she had always been protected and in fact, this was the first time during her stay in Goa, that she had ventured out on her own.

The thought of being pregnant terrified her. She had been a virgin until this time. Paula had vowed not to lose her virginity until her wedding night, when she would have offered herself to her one and only true love.

Many troubling questions destroyed her peace now. "What would I say to Dona Herodiana if she found out? What would Lino feel if he came to know that it is his child in my womb? What would the villagers think of their beloved Dona Paula? How will I break this news to my dear mother? How would she live through this shame of her daughter bearing a child out of wedlock?"

Not a soul stirred. A couple of times, her heart did pound hard when an aggressive dog came too close to her, threatening to bite however, a swing of her case sent it yelping away.

As Paula walked briskly onward, praying that the direction she was taking was correct, she soon found herself at the river's edge. Paula had reached the banks of the River Mandovi. The water shimmered in the soft glow of the moonlight. The lapping sound of the water against the rocky bank calmed her disturbed soul. She continued to urge her tired feet upriver. Distraught with feelings of futility and confusion, she decided to sit at a makeshift pier that some fishermen had built.

As Paula wrangled with the tumult of life-draining thoughts of guilt and frustration, her brain became numb and she stared blankly at the bobbing canoe moored to the side of the pier. As if in a trance, she delicately stepped into the canoe and loosened it from its moorings. Paula made no attempt to recover her suitcase. She watched it getting smaller and smaller as the current took control of the canoe and her fate. Paula laid her head on a bundle of fishing nets inside the boat and slipped into a deep slumber.

Lino was very upset when the panic stricken McKenna's, came to tell him of her disappearance and the parting note that gave no indication of where she was going. "Where are you, my beloved?" the shocked Lino asked himself, over and over again.

It was now noon and there was still no sign of Paula. Lino was very concerned. Once again he searched the quarry to see if she had left any message but there was none. He could not see her leather case either. He cringed at the thought of Paula getting discovered by the Inquisition. Pushing the thought aside, he looked for the suitcase everywhere but it could not be located. By now it was late evening. Already she had been saved once before from sure death. He was very concerned about not knowing who Padre Ivo's accomplice was. Who could it be and why would he do such a thing? Where could she have gone? He wondered if the exhibition of his love for Paula had left her confused and fearful of him. Could he be responsible for her decision to flee?

The captain had confided in Pedro about Paula being alive and the danger that surrounded her. He too joined in the search but left the Captain to do the searching in the woods while he decided to visit the fishing village nearby. Nearing the Mandovi, he saw Menino, an old fisherman mending his net on a wooden pier. Lino greeted him and told him about Paula's disappearance. Menino's hands froze in mid-action as he mended the tear in the net and stared at Pedro wide-eyed. He told Pedro about the leather bag that he had found on the pier and the disappearance of his canoe. He had handed it over to the Chaplain. Although Menino's son had searched the river and its banks for the missing canoe from morning till evening, it was nowhere to be found.

Pedro's heart grew heavy as he raced his bicycle to the chapel. It had grown dark and the bells were tolling for the evening prayer. The chaplain was praying his Angelus inside the chapel. Pedro waited for him to finish his prayer and met him as he was leaving. Pedro was hoping and praying that the suitcase would not be Paula's. Tears rolled down his eyes when he saw the worn leather bag, which he identified as being Paula's the moment he had set his eyes on it. There was nothing in it except Paula's clothes and a frame with a portrait of her parents. But he had missed checking the secret compartment, which contained her journal. Dejected and totally shaken up by Paula's disappearance, his thoughts wandered to a canoe, somewhere out there on the high seas. He told himself that there still was hope that it was afloat and could be found with Paula alive and whole.

That night Pedro and Ana kept up a night vigil in front of the little altar in their home, storming heaven's doors with their fervent prayers.

...❦♦❧...

The Captain's posse had returned without luck. Lino spent a sleepless night, seeing nightmares of his dear Paula. Just as his tired, heavy eyes finally closed just minutes before sunrise, the continuous rapping of the door knocker rudely awakened him. Herodiana just groaned and turned on her side totally oblivious to what was happening.

The Captain almost sleepwalked to the front door and struggled to find the *"adambo"*, and to dislodge it from its locked position. He was surprised as well as irritated that Maria the maid had responded to the knocking.

Standing on the porch were two Portuguese police officers who had brought with them a fisherman who was holding something in his hand. There was no doubt that the coat, which the fisherman was holding up for his identification, was his. The police explained in Portuguese that it was found snagged to a capsized canoe, by a fishing boat returning to shore with their nights catch.

The soft, silken sand of Morjim beach was home to a million little crabs dashing out of holes and scrambling to the sea, some doing the exact opposite. The beach was riddled with their little holes undisturbed by man. The somnolent rays of the rising sun illuminated the polished sea-shells, beautifully sculpted by God, making them appear like sparkling diamonds strewn all over the beach. A few seagulls circled the waters in search of food. The forest of tall, snaky coconut palms seemed to compete with each other to touch the slowly brightening skies. Somewhere in the distance, a rooster was crowing. It was about time the women got ready to meet their tired husbands and relieve them of their catch.

Under the whitewashed cross atop a cluster of rocks built by the fishermen to protect them from the perils of the sea, something stirred in the sand. It was a woman with her body caked with wet sand, almost camouflaged. The eyelids fluttered briefly and finally opened. She seemed to test each limb for movement and satisfied that her body was responding, wondered where she was. Feeling very weak and using one of the damp rocks for support, she eased herself up and brushed the sand off her clothes and face. She was soon gripped with fear of being the only human on the beach, but the presence of melted wax on the cross meant that there was a village nearby. The swim to the shore after her canoe had capsized had drained her of all strength. At first she had made no effort to save herself but then she remembered what the Holy Bible had written about life. "God has created me in His likeness and image. God has a great plan for my life. In the book of Jeremiah, he has promised me a hope and a future". She could barely walk. Resting her head against the foot of the cross, she lost consciousness again.

Soon the beach was filled with voices. About a score of women in colourful blouses and cotton saris pulled up and tucked back into the small of the back, lined up on the beach with bamboo baskets balancing on their heads. One of the dogs which had followed them down to the beach, silenced their chatter by looking towards the cross and barking incessantly. The figure at the cross was rudely awakened by the noise.

The women by now had gathered around her, curious about what a *'firangi'* was doing in their part of the world. The arrival of their husbands' boats interrupted their investigation and they all decided to come back after they had loaded their baskets with the catch. Paula clutched the warm cup of tea which a kind woman had poured out from a *'bulho'* and watched the dark-skinned, muscular, loin-covered men expertly push their craft on oiled logs onto the upper part of the beach, away from the high tide line. The nets were laden with fish, both large and small. The women went about the chores of sorting the fish according to their size and type, momentarily forgetting about the strange lady.

Meanwhile, in Oddavel, the memorial service for Paula was attended by Lino, Herodiana, Pedro, Ana, Maria, Jaku, Linda, Andrew, Padre Ivo and a few close friends of the Captain. As the priest did his best to deliver a touching homily about how no one was too young to die and how Paula had lived a wonderful Christian life, the Captain's thoughts wandered off to how Paula, from that first day at the Abranches mansion, had filled his heart with warmth. Herodiana had initially swept him off his feet with her beauty and aristocratic bearing however she had failed to keep her marital vows. Every attempt at convincing her or coaxing her to bear children had failed miserably. Being a catholic and respected member of the Portuguese society in Goa, he was loathe to think of divorce, although his marriage to Herodiana was long dead. They kept up appearances to keep the gossip down and lived together like they were guests. The servants, of course, had sensed that much was amiss. Herodiana's sharp tongue and mood swings had made her unpopular. The Captain reminisced about how attracted he was to Paula's talent in painting and great conversations that they'd had as she painted. He had discovered in Paula a soul mate; someone he wished would replace Herodiana in his dreary life. His harmless attraction to Paula had, over the months, grown into a fatal one. It had bonded them into timeless lovers, signing almost in blood; an unbreakable pact, a secret well kept from Herodiana and all others.

Lino had changed his desire to die fighting, to a passion to live; live only for Paula. His reverie was disturbed by an elbow jab from Herodiana reminding him that it was time to stand for the final blessing.

"No! My beloved has not died" his heart screamed. "Unless I have proof of her death, I will continue to believe that she is alive!"

The women had already conveyed the 'firangi's' presence to their men. As the fishermen trudged upto the cross to offer their thanksgiving prayers. Paula, who was now standing and watching the activity on the beach, wished them *"Bom Dia"* in Portuguese. Although their parents were converted to Christianity by the Portuguese missionaries who came from the City of Goa, the fisher-folk still spoke their native language Konkani; however Isidore, an elderly man who had worked in the city at the docks, knew Portuguese. He stepped forward and asked her name.

She answered weakly, "Paula". She then surprised them with her story told in broken Konkani, a story close to the truth but not the whole truth as she decided to keep the pregnancy a secret.

Isidore lived alone with his wife, Bella. They were childless but even in their advanced age, they were both blest with good health and happiness. Bella had taken a liking to Paula from the first sight. She found Paula's innocence and youth very appealing and at once insisted that she share their dwelling with them. Supporting Paula between them, they walked slowly towards the settlement hidden within a dense coconut grove.

The trek to the village took close to half an hour. The women with their fish-laden baskets, chatting with their husbands, made a pretty sight against the background of the dense palm-fringed higher ground. Enroute, they passed through numerous thatched boat shelters, which were used only in the monsoons when fishing was simply not possible. The monsoon season was a slack season for the fishermen. This was a time for mending their nets or preparing new nets for the fishing season ahead. Soon, they were walking through a dense forest of palms. Nestled in the palms were several quaint mud houses with sloping roofs covered with thatched roofs. Almost every house had a small cross outside the house and a fenced garden full of flowering plants.

The tired fishermen headed off to their homes for a much deserved sleep whilst the ladies proceeded toward the market to sell the mornings catch at the *'tinto'*. Bella had to request a neighbor to take care of selling her share of the fish as she decided to stay back to care for Paula.

Isidore and Bella's humble abode was neatly kept. The lean-to roof at the entrance covered a small verandah which was raised on a plinth, accessed via a flight of six steps. On each side of the verandah was a wooden bench. The floor as well as the walls was covered with cow-dung which gave the house a light-green look. The sturdy entrance door was made of teakwood. As Isidore opened the door, Paula saw the beautifully decorated, carved altar, housing the 'holy family' on the wall in front of her. The earthen lamps lit by Bella for her morning prayer for the safe return of her husband were still burning.

Isidore showed her around the small house beginning with the kitchen which consisted of a small bathing area with a large brass pot next to it. The pot was placed on 3 stones with firewood placed beneath. The small hatch left in the wall of the bath was for reaching into the brass pot with a tumbler to draw water out for bathing. Immediately next to the bath was an elevated mud structure holding three fire places with earthen pots kept ready for cooking. Under the platform was a store for firewood, well stocked with dry twigs and palm fronds. On the corner of the same platform was placed a slab of black granite stone with a stone roller. This was their grinding stone, to make coconut paste for their curry. A square table with four home-made chairs was their dining table. There was a single bedroom with a bamboo weave mat that was rolled up and kept standing in the corner. A couple of wooden chests held their clothes. A beautifully carved rosewood wardrobe with a mirror on one of its doors stood against a wall.

"This", Bella explained sighing and giving a loving glance at Isidore, "was part of my 'dowry' when we got married".

The living room had a few wood-framed chairs with cane netting on the seats and backs. The centre table was also made of wood frame with cane netting. The translucent shell covered windows were shut and the sunlight although blocked, was making the white shell platelets glow like white pearls letting in a soft glow inside the room. Isidore opened the windows and at once cool sea-breeze filled the interiors. Paula was tired and so was Isidore. He made the bed for Paula on the floor of the inner room whilst he slept in the verandah. Bella retired to her kitchen, to prepare an elaborate lunch for their guest.

When Isidore and Bella were first told of the pregnancy, they were curious to know who the father of the baby was. Aware of their curiosity, Paula told them about Lino. But she did so only after pleading with them to keep it a secret from the rest of the village, lest it leaked out to someone malicious.

A few months later, it was time for Paula to have the baby. She was really showing now and sleep wouldn't come easily specially on a mat with just a hand sewn quilt as mattress. The villagers were told a convincing story by Bella. According to her story, Paula had been coerced by her vile husband to abort her baby but she had refused to do so. Having no option but to run from him, in her desperation, she had decided to escape in a canoe which had capsized close to their shores.

Paula missed her soft, comfortable bed and the loving care of her dear mother in Portugal. Adeline, the village midwife had already assessed Paula's condition and had told Bella that she could expect the baby very soon. The baby had descended low in her womb and appeared to be positioned for the delivery.

Adeline was the only midwife available in the village. Although the village depended on her skills at midwifery handed down to her from her ancestors, Adeline herself had no children and always longed for a child of her own. Her husband was a waster and a drunk who had left her. It was rumoured that he had taken his own life.

When Paula was brought to her for a routine checkup, she was baffled by Paula's wish to give up her baby for adoption when she was born. Not wanting to probe into Paula's life, she resisted from asking her to give the baby to her only out of fear of Isidore and Bella. Adeline knew that the old couple would never allow Paula to give up her baby.

One night, Isidore and Bella returned early to bed. It was Isidore's night off from fishing and after chatting with Bella and Paula, had dozed off in Bella's lap. It wasn't long after, when Bella also decided to call it a night. Paula tossed and turned on her hard mat on the floor. Bella had lovingly stitched a quilt out of left-over fabric which she had collected from the village tailor. It helped soften her bed but she longed for her soft cotton mattress. The fumigation with incense did not do much to chase out the mosquitoes and without a mosquito net, they feasted on her blood.

Paula suddenly became still. She could feel the baby moving. She placed her hands on her big belly and followed the movement. It felt like a knee or an elbow pushing out at her belly. "O Lino! How I wish you were here beside me, to help me bring this baby into this world together. I wonder what you would have said had I to tell you of our baby. But alas! Neither you nor I will ever be able to enjoy the fruit of our love".

Paula pulled out the priceless shawl from under her pillow and wrapped it around each palm and brought it up to her lips and kissed it. She had lost her coat but fortunately, the shawl was still around her neck when she was washed to the shore that fateful night. Burying her face in the shawl, she managed to shut her eyes for a while. But the first pangs of labour jolted her awake. It was an excruciating, stretching pain that seemed to travel to her back and soon reduce in intensity until it completely left her. Half an hour later the pain returned. The frequency of the labour pain was now increasing. Paula called out to Bella and Isidore. At first, neither heard her until Paula crawled over to where they were sleeping and gently shook them awake. The painful expression on Paula's face said it all. Isidore was up and out of the house, as fast as his feeble legs could carry him, while Bella rushed to the kitchen to put some water on the stove. She also made a concoction out of some herbs and boiled it over another stove. It was an age-old herbal drink that all the women of the village knew about. It would help to lightly sedate the woman during the delivery and give her some relief from the pain. Bella held the cup to Paula's lips and made sure she consumed the entire portion. Soon, the neighbours were alerted of the situation and four able bodied men placed Paula on a makeshift stretcher and raced her to the midwife's house.

Adeline was ready for the birthing, as Isidore had pedaled frantically ahead of the stretcher-bearers to tell her to be prepared. When Paula was brought there, Adeline insisted on being left alone with Paula inside the room, except for her sister, who would assist with the delivery. Isidore, Bella and the others remained outside, praying.

Soon, from inside, the baby spluttered and then coughed lightly and gave out a loud cry. Almost immediately after the first cry, there was another loud cry.

Tears turned to gladness and Isidore lit a fuse to a single *'fozno'* to announce to the village that a girl was born to Paula! Burning two would have signaled the arrival of a boy. This was a custom that was prevalent in almost all parts of Goa. A nervous and suspicious looking Adeline came outside to report that both mother and child were declared safe and out of danger. Although Isidore and Bella could not understand the tension on Adeline's face, they soon brushed the thought aside as they rushed inside to hug the sweating Paula, who lay caressing her baby on her breast.

When little Paulina was about two months old, the threat of smallpox hung over Morjim. The village was grieving over two children and a woman who had already died from the deadly pestilence. Isidore and Bella were full of concern for Paula and her child.

"My child, you will have to go to the City. Please understand we are not chasing you out but for Paulina's sake, you will have to go", Isidore told her one day. Bella sat in a corner silently shedding tears.

It broke Paula's heart to leave them, but she knew that she had to leave. She had to go to the City, for she had plans to keep her child at the *Recolhimento de Nossa Senhora de Serra*, which looked after orphans. That was because she wanted to stay at the Santa Monica Convent until her baby was big enough for them to make a trip to Portugal.

When he was working on the docks, Isidore had helped another young lady in distress. Now this woman was a nun in the Convent of Santa Monica. On the previous day, he had paid her a visit and to his delight had found out that Sr. Magdalena de Santa Cruz was presently the acting Prioress there. He had told her the story of Paula and asked for her help. The kind nun had reassured him that Paula could stay at the convent.

So the next day, Paula was ready to leave. Bella and Paula had cried the whole night long; in fact even Isidore had not slept well. Paula knew that she would have to part from this old couple but she had never thought that it would be this early. But with her inner reserves of strength and her faith in the Almighty's providence, she accepted this new situation.

She hugged Bella, and cried in her arms for a long time. Isidore arranged a horse-driven carriage for her and he was going to make the trip to the City with her.

"I shall pray everyday that all your dreams will eventually come true", the old woman assured her.

Paula and little Paulina took Bella's blessings and those of the other elderly people of the village. She had hoped that Adeline would be there, but for some reason she did not turn up. Then waving a tearful goodbye to the villagers assembled there, Paula climbed into the carriage. Tears flowed down her cheeks as the tiny village slowly disappeared from sight.

Chapter 11

CONVENT OF SANTA MONICA

Annabel de Vasconceles was 55 years of age. She was a strong-willed person, who had conquered the tragedies and faults of a painful past to become an understanding and sensitive person. She looked tough on the outside but she had a very soft and gentle heart and was always concerned about others. Annabel had not allowed her past to embitter her. In fact, it had mellowed her down and made her a sweet and gentle person. However she did feel the pain of a jilted lover and her lost child. She was tall and graceful, with a ready smile. She had good features, which showed that she was really beautiful in her younger days. However, she had a long scar on her right cheek.

Annabel came from a devout Christian family. Her father was an assistant commander on a naval ship, which was sunk by pirates while sailing to Africa. Barely a year after her father's death, Annabel lost her mother at the age of six. She was considered as an *Orfa Del Rei* and was sent down to Goa in 1630 at the age of 18. But fate was very cruel to young Annabel. She was the most beautiful girl among the 12, which were sent that year. However, she almost lost her life when she was trying to save one of the girls who was entangled in the rigging ropes when the ship was fighting bad weather at sea. At that moment one of poles holding the sails broke free and fell on her. She survived the accident but her left cheek was badly scared.

When the ship finally reached Goa, Annabel recovered from her wounds but the scar on her face eliminated all chances of marriage. No one wanted to marry her! Then she met Constancio, a Portuguese clerk who pretended to be in love with her. He managed to coax her into sleeping with him. He had promised to marry her but once he had satisfied his lust, he left her. When she was just recovering from a broken heart, two months later, she had discovered that she was pregnant.

As an *Orfa Del Rei*, she was still entitled to the dowry promised by the King. Realising this, another man wanted to marry her but she refused when he suggested that she should abort the baby. When she finally had the baby, one of her fellow *Orfaas del Rei* who was happily married to an army officer coaxed her to give the baby to the *Recolhimento de Nossa Senhora de Serra*, but she was refused as they felt that she was able enough to support the child herself.

Annabel had to bring up the child alone. However those were not the times when a single mother could really survive in society. The same man, who wanted her to abort the baby, paid some assassins to attack the tiny cottage near the seaside where she lived with her baby boy. In the scuffle that ensued, the baby suffered a blow on the head as she tripped and fell to the ground whilst escaping from the assailants. Her friend Rosalind cared for her and her injured child but they could not save the child who succumbed to his injuries.

The grief was unbearable and Rosalind convinced Annabel to stay at the *Recolhimento de Maria Magdalena* where she surrendered her sorrows to the Lord and spent her days in prayer. Eventually, she joined the Monastery of Santa Monica and took a new name, Sr. Magdalena De Santa Cruz. The Convent of Santa Monica was completed in 1627. It was the first convent in Portuguese-Asia, located next to the Our Lady of Grace Church and the school of Our Lady of Populo and St. Augustine. Women of noble birth who joined were given a black veil and called *madres* or choir sisters. The others were given a white veil and were called sisters or *sorores*. They wore a habit of rough cotton material in the form of a white tunic gathered at the waist with a black leather belt. The head was covered with a scarf.

Annabel was respected by everyone for her piety and not just preached religion but also practiced it. She was always kind and considerate towards the other inmates specially with the non-European nuns who joined the convent.

Isidore, Paula and her child arrived at the Convent of Santa Monica in the afternoon that day. Fortunately for them, Sr. Magdalene de Santa Cruz was very sympathetic when Paula explained to her all that had happened, keeping out the name of the child's father.

"My child, I will do my best to help you", she said to Paula.

"Madre, I don't want to be a hindrance to your convent life. I brought this child into this world because I had no right to kill her before she was born. But now I know that sometime or another, I will have to give this child away. That is because the father of this child lives in this city. If he ever finds me I don't want him to know about the child. It would greatly jeopardise matters for him. Madre, please do me another favour. I know a place where she will be taken care of. But for that I need your help", she said with tears welling up in her eyes.

Sr. Magdalena listened patiently and then she told Paula that she understood her predicament.

"My child, I understand what you are going through because I faced a similar problem. I was an Orfa Del Rei. I was sent in the second batch of orphans dispatched from Portugal as a prospective bride to Portuguese men living in Goa. That was to maintain a European identity and increase the European population in this region. But alas, an accident scarred my face. No one wanted to marry me thereafter", she explained, pausing to catch her breath.

"Then, I met a man who told me that he loved me and wanted to marry me. I trusted him so much that I did not refuse even my body to him, but later I realized that he was just using me. I was pregnant with his child, but I had no one to help me. I managed to give birth to a baby boy although he was against the idea of me keeping the baby. Then I thought I would look after him alone. However that didn't work. There were too many vultures in society waiting to pounce on me. And then one day, I was attacked by some horrible men, who may have been sent by my ex-lover, and my baby . . ." She broke into tears, the past still haunting her.

Paula, put an arm around her and kissed her cheek.

"I am sorry, Madre. Your experience is far sadder than mine. I understand now why you are in a position to sympathise with me. Madre, I heard that the *Recolhimento de Nossa Senhora de Serra* keeps orphans. Isn't it true?"

"Yes it does, child. In fact, I had spoken to them about my own little boy. But it was too late", she stated, breaking into sobs again.

"It will break my heart Madre, but I will have to do that with Paulina. I know that the government takes care of the orphans there. But Madre, promise that you will help me get her back when I arrange a passage back to Portugal", said Paula, her voice trembling with the sorrow of the decision.

"I will do my best to get her back for you. I will also do my best to send you both to Portugal", promised Sr. Magdalena.

A month passed since Paula had moved to the Monastery of Santa Monica. She cooked and mopped for the Madres. The local nuns who could be distinguished by the white veils they wore, helped to take care of little Paulina. Sr. Magdalena was very kind to her too.

Then one night, Sr. Magdalena informed her that the new Prioress had arrived and was presently at the port of Cochin. "She will be here soon. But don't worry, I have spoken to the Regente of the orphanage. They will put it up to the *Mesa*, which is the committee governing the two *Recolhimentos*. I will take the baby to them for I have not disclosed that you are living here", she told Paula.

That night Paula didn't sleep a wink. She held little Paulina close to her and sobbed bitterly. Early that morning, Sister Magdalena came to take the baby away.

Paula prayed on her knees to the Lord to give her strength. And that morning she felt God's grace to part with her baby. So at the age of four months, little Paulina was sent to the orphanage.

...⋙♦⋘...

Paula's life took an uncomplicated routine at the convent. She woke up at 5 a.m. every morning. She had a cup of simple tea and hurried towards the chapel for mass at 7 a.m. After mass, she sat in the library reading.

Later in the day, she spent her time, working in the vegetable garden. She had also cultivated a flower patch, which she looked after personally.

The *surours* lived a very hard life and subjected themselves to rigorous fasts, night vigils, heavy work and loneliness of perpetual cloister. Some of the sisters were very good at needlework and sweets. These were sold in the market and helped with the income of the place. Some were talented poets and wrote graceful verses.

Paula had a small room with a simple bed, a table and a stool. The servants and slaves had separate dormitories.

The Royal Monastry of St. Monica was far from poor. It owned paddy fields and palm groves and collected rents from properties and houses received as dowries from the parents of the nuns when they joined the convent and also donations received for prayers offered by the nuns.

Two years had passed now; Paula led a life of a recluse in the huge Monastery. Giving up the baby had been a blow to her. She had met Isidore and Bella only twice after their parting, since the rules for outsiders visiting the convent were made more stringent.

From them, she came to know that many children from that village had died of the small pox. They also informed her that Adeline had disappeared from Morjim, soon after she had left.

"Paula, my Paula! How can I ever forget you?" lamented Lino, as he passed the quarry where he and Paula had spent so many happy days together. Over three years had passed but his heart had never accepted that she was dead. They say time is the best healer, but it was not so for the poor Captain.

"I am sorry, Paula. I know I shouldn't have encouraged this relationship at all", he wept, as he rode out of the forest. He often went hunting alone when the sadness became unbearable.

It was July, and the monsoons that year were at their worst. As Lino was returning home, a thunderstorm hit the place. He rode on despite the pouring rain. But suddenly lightning struck a tree in front of him. Luckily, his mount instinctively reared up on its two legs, as a huge branch crashed right in front of them. But the animal slipped in the soft clay, and both, horse and rider fell heavily.

When Lino got up, he realised that the horse had injured its leg and didn't know what to do. At that moment he saw some lights through the trees. He walked slowly towards the place. In the darkness and the thundering rain, he didn't know exactly where he was. But right now that was unimportant.

Surprisingly the gate was open, so he went inside and knocked on the big door. A woman in a flowing robe opened the door for him. She recognized the insignia on his garment and knew that he was of high bearing.

"Ma'am, I know I am troubling you, but can you please let me keep my horse in your stables?" he asked her.

"Don't worry Sir, no one should be out in this merciless weather. Keep the horse in and come down to the guest room for some hot soup. I will have it sent down to you", she told him politely.

"Thank you, Madre", he told her, realising for the first time that he was in a convent. He was still feeling a little dazed from the fall.

After washing his bruised elbows and his knee in the washroom, he sat down at the small meagerly furnished room which had a table and two chairs. But what caught his interest was a painting of a saintly lady on the wall adjacent to the door. As he was admiring it, a young woman dressed in a nun's habit entered the room with hot soup. He heard her only when the soup bowl rattled on the tray she was carrying.

When he turned around, he smiled at her but she had already turned to go back.

"Thank you very much for your kindness, Madre", he called after. Then observing that she had dropped some soup on her hands, he added, "Madre are you hurt? Let me have a look at it". But the young nun mumbled an *'Obrigado'* (thanks) and hurried out of the door.

"Poor girl, must be scared of men. God bless her", said the captain, when he heard her footsteps growing fainter.

The soup had made him feel better. He had removed his jacket and squeezed it dry. Then he moved to the window, which opened out into the backyard. The rain had stopped for a brief moment. There was a bolt of lightning, which illuminated the whole yard before him. In the brilliant light, Lino saw something, which made his heart pound like a galloping horse. In the verandah of an outhouse, which could be seen from the window, he had seen a familiar looking multi-colored shawl drying out on a clothesline.

Paula had run into her room and shut the door. Her heart was doing all sorts of crazy things and her chest was heaving as she breathed hard. She huddled into a corner with her face buried in her knees, as large sobs racked her body.

When Sr. Magdalena asked her to serve a man who had sought refuge from the rain, little did she know what was in store for her.

After the arrival of the new Prioress, Sr. Magdalena was made the deputy and was kept in charge of the younger inmates of the Convent, something which suited Paula well.

Paula recognized the Captain from his very stance, as he stood admiring the painting of Santa Monica. Thankfully the door had been open and she had enough time to avoid his attention when she was laying the soup on the table. When he turned around, her knees were trembling and that was when she had quickly turned to avoid getting recognized. Luckily he had not seen her face.

"Lino, Lino! What should I do now Lord?" she went on crying out.

Suddenly she heard a knock on the door. She hurriedly wiped her eyes dry and opened the door. And there in front of her was Lino, looking as pale as a ghost. In his hand he was clutching the shawl, which he had given her.

"Paula. O Paula! Oh God!" he said, falling at her feet and kissing her. He rose just in time to catch Paula as she fainted. He hugged her passionately and wanted to kiss her, but her vest and habit stopped him from giving vent to his feelings.

"I am sorry . . ." he said abashedly although he knew she was not listening. He gently laid her on her cot just as someone pushed the door open. It was an angry looking Sr. Magdalena.

"Sir is this the way you repay our hospitality?" she asked, then glancing at the tear-stained, sleeping Paula, she added with iciness creeping into her voice, "What have you done to her?"

Luckily for Lino, Paula recovered at that very moment and taken in the scene before her.

"Madre . . .", she cried weakly.

"My child, are you alright? Has this evil man harmed you?" she asked turning to Paula, with concern in her voice.

"Madre, it is not how it may appear to you. I know this man and he hasn't done anything wrong to me. He is the man I told you about", Paula told her, sobbing bitterly.

"I am sorry, Sir", Sr. Magdalena apologized to Lino.

But the Captain smiled at her. "Madre, I am the one who should apologize. It is not your fault at all. In fact I have no right to be in her chambers", he said.

He then explained to Sr. Magdalena who he was and all that had happened. The Captain's humility and genuineness touched her heart.

"Have I lost Paula forever to this religious life she has chosen or would she want me to take her back?" He asked hopefully.

From the talk it was obvious that he didn't know about the little Paulina. That information had to be kept from him at any cost.

Turning to Lino Sr. Magdalena said, "Sir I leave you to talk things over with her. But don't take too long".

When they were alone again, Lino broke into sobs, "I am sorry, Paula. I am guilty of ruining your life. Please forgive me for taking advantage of you. I perfectly understand that you wanted to escape from me", he said, kneeling in front of her.

"Please rise my Lord. There is nothing to be forgiven. I can't bear to see you this way. I . . . l . . . l . . ." she said and paused in mid-sentence.

"Please say it, Paula. Tell me what I have longed to hear. Please say it. I had thought I had lost you forever".

"I love you . . ." said Paula, her sobs now shaking her whole body.

Lino moved towards her, still kneeling and took her hands in his and kissed them.

"Please Paula, won't you come back with me? Please or I will die", he said and then quoted a verse from the poem she had written for him when he had rescued her,

Yours till the end of life

Every breath, every heartbeat

Every thought, every dream

Mind, body and soul

My love, I offer unto thee

Paula was silent. So Lino pleaded with her again, "Please come home Paula. I promise you will be safe there now. Padre Ivo has been caught by the inquisition and is facing the death penalty for impersonating a priest. I will tell you all about it later. If Dona Herodiana troubles you, I will talk to the McKennas and keep you there till I work things out".

Paula just looked down at him lovingly yet made no move to go with him. After a long speechless while, the captain decided to leave Paula alone, hoping she would make up her mind about coming back.

"The rain has stopped, and so I must leave", the Captain said, his heart on fire, as he gazed at Paula. Then he turned around, walked out of the door, towards a small rear door of the guest room.

...❧◆❧...

When the Captain left, Sr. Magdalena couldn't bear to see her beloved Paula sobbing bitterly.

"My child . . . I know you still love him so much. Why are you torturing yourself?" she asked her, "You told me that his wife has aborted his babies and doesn't love him. Isn't it true that she has a lover?"

"That is true, Madre . . . but I didn't tell him about that yet. Madre, I didn't want his family name to be put to shame".

"But my child, do you think that it is fair that the Captain suffers so much? He seems to be a very good man. And from what you told me he has suffered enough. Go to him. I think your happiness lies with him. But it is your decision. Decide fast before he leaves. Meanwhile I will delay him at the gate", said Sr. Magdalena, going out of the room.

"Tell him that I still love him", Paula cried.

As the Captain was leading his horse to the gate, he saw the old nun waving out to him to stop. He hesitated and then went up to her. She was breathing hard as she hurried to meet him halfway.

"What are you doing about Paula?"

"What do you mean Madre? She is a nun and she belongs here now. I respect her decision", said the Captain, trying to keep his voice steady.

"No, my son, things are not as they look", said Sr. Magdalena, "She still loves you. That's what she told me as you left".

The Captain froze. The old nun was a little confused at his reaction. "Why Captain, don't you love her anymore", she asked.

"I do, Madre", he said after a long pause.

"But then, isn't it un-Christian to love another woman, when God has put you and your wife together?" she asked. The Captain was confused at this statement. Now he was not sure on whose side this kind nun was.

"Madre, according to the Church, I think my marriage will be considered null and void, as I have now found proof that my wife never wants to have children and that she has aborted her babies . . . my babies", he told her with tears in his eyes, for recently he had also found out that she had undergone a treatment so that she would never conceive again.

"Then what have you decided to do?" she asked him.

"Madre, I also know that my wife has a lover who comes to the villa. One day I have planned to catch them in the act. After that, I will divorce her and marry Paula", he confided in her.

"In that case Captain, you have my blessings. You can take Paula if she desires to go with you", she told him, shaking his hand and smiling. She had been testing him and was happy with his answers.

...❧◆❧...

When the Captain entered her room a second time that night, Paula was lying on her bed not getting any sleep over what had happened earlier. She thought that it was Sr. Magdalena who had entered the room.

"Has the Captain gone Madre?" she asked, in between sobs.

"How can he go without you?" he said tenderly. And Paula looked up in astonishment.

"Lino, it is you!" she exclaimed and hid her face in her hands.

The Captain went over to her in the corner and lifted her up gently. Taking her in his arms, he kissed her on her forehead. "Come, my love, let us go home now if you so desire. But we will have to keep our relationship under cover for at least a month", he told her, explaining his plan.

"I will do anything to keep our secret safe", she said earnestly. Now the Captain was not sure whether he should suggest the other alternative he had in mind. He wanted to tell her that she could stay in the convent until he had settled with Herodiana.

Sr. Magdalena entered the room at that time. "So what have you decided my child?" she asked.

"Madre, I want to go if I have your permission", she said hugging the nun.

"Come now my child, tomorrow after mass, we will speak to the Prioress. Don't worry I will explain to her", she reassured her.

"Paula, do you want to stay here till everything is settled? That would save you from meeting with Herodiana again", she said.

"Thank you Madre for your concern. I would gladly take the insults from Dona Herodiana only to be close to Lino again ", Paula told her with a smile.

Sr. Magdalena was happy that the girl who she had grown to love so much was so mature in her thinking.

So early next morning, an excited Pedro and Ana came to escort Paula home. The sight made Paula remember that first day at the dock. "Would the Captain ride down to welcome her, as he did on that first day?" she wondered, smiling at those happy memories.

"Paula my child", exclaimed Pedro. Ana was sobbing loudly and praising God. The old couple embraced her and they wept for joy.

She waved goodbye to Sr. Magdalena who had come to the gate. She had already bid farewell to the other sisters, who were all sad to see her go. Of course, they didn't know anything more than that. Before leaving her room, she had spoken to Sr. Magdalena giving her instructions about her child.

"Madre, I thank you for all your kindness, and especially because you kept my secret. I will come for the child once my mother sends me her blessings and all is clear for the Captain, "she told the old nun.

"Don't worry Paula, I promise to help you get the child back when you tell me to", Sr. Magdalena promised, embracing her.

"Madre, also tell *Tia* Bella and *Tio* Isidore where I am. Tell them that I am happy and will go to see them once everything is settled", she requested.

...࿓◆࿓...

That evening Herodiana was very impatient and irritated. She had just taken out her frustration on Preta. For all these years, even the few slaves bought by the Abranches household had been treated like any of the other 'free' men and women working there. Until she joined the household, it was obvious that her irritation stemmed from the fact that Lino was at home. Though she didn't want him to be close to her any longer, she was jealous that he was so visibly affected by Paula's disappearance.

"Thank god we put her out of the way", she thought, priding herself of the well thought-out plan to get Paula in trouble. At the same time, the thought of Padre Ivo's capture by the Inquisition made matters very difficult for both Amorous and her. What if he talked about their involvement in getting Paula in trouble?

As she gazed out of her balcony, she suddenly heard a commotion below.

"Preta, come here!" She shouted out to her slave.

The poor girl came running in. "*Senhora*, what is it? What can I do for you?" she asked.

"Go find out what all that noise is about".

The slave girl ran down the stairs and came back in a few minutes, breathing hard with the effort.

"*Senhora*, Dona Paula back !" she exclaimed.

Just then there was a shout from downstairs, "Paula is back!"

"Oh no!" roared Herodiana with rage. Then she grabbed the poor slave girl and slapped her so hard that she reeled and fell to the ground unconscious. Kicking her in the stomach, Herodiana stepped over her and went down the stairs, shouting "Praise the Lord for he has indeed done something magnificent!"

Lino and Paula, who had just entered the parlour, looked up. Both had surprised looks on their faces. The latter was taken aback by the warm welcome she received from her employer.

"Paula, my girl, where have you been? I missed you so much", she said, hugging Paula who was totally baffled at all this emotion.

...᠅◆᠅...

So Paula was re-installed as Herodiana's lady-in-waiting. As the days passed by, she saw the angry glances that her mistress threw her way. All that love, which she had showed on that first day, was just an eyewash.

But Paula, the tender and ever-forgiving person that she was, took all this in her stride. Now she felt a new strength within her to bear all this. She knew that Lino loved her. She no longer felt guilty that she was in love with him.

"My child, you are the best thing that ever happened to my gentle master. He deserves you and in fact he lives because of the love that you have installed in his heart". Pedro's words kept reverberating in her heart.

However, she didn't misuse the knowledge of her master's love, to make her bitter towards Herodiana. She continued serving her with all humility. That night she went through all the mail she had received from Portugal. The following three nights were spent replying to her mother's letters. She wrote that she was fine but because of some problems with the mail, she was unable to answer for the last few years. In her letters she praised the Abranches household, including Herodiana. Pedro had given her back her suitcase and at once she had checked to see if her old diary was still intact. She felt a strong urge to note down everything that had transpired. It would take her a lot of time to write it all but nevertheless, she began recording everything in the diary whenever time permitted.

On the fourth night, as she opened and read the last of her mail, she burst into tears. Her dear old nanny, Catherine had died a year ago. The news was unbearable. Paula ran down to Pedro and informed him about his aunt's passing. And he consoled her as she sobbed bitterly.

Paula realised why Lino was avoiding her. Her heart filled with sorrow. "Till when Lord?" she wondered. But then, she realised that maybe he was still feeling guilty that he had made love to her. As promised, he stayed away from her though he couldn't bear to do so. He couldn't bear the guilt and pressure any longer and decided to volunteer for another campaign.

Pedro who heard about it informed Paula.

"My child, it is now or never. You have to settle Lino's mind. I am sure he still feels responsible for your going away. But then you have to be bold if you really love him", he told her.

As Lino was all set to leave the house for headquarters that morning, Pedro whispered to him that Paula was not in the house.

"Sir, lately the men have seen some cobras around the hill", he said, "I hope she hasn't gone up to the hill".

Now nothing could hold him back. Pedro smiled as he saw the captain mount his horse and shoot off towards the hillock. The plan had worked. On second thoughts, he had not told him a lie. There had been python sightings in the area close to the hillock.

The Captain found Paula near the hillside. She was sketching the beautiful landscape which was spread out in front of her. On the horizon, the sea was transformed into a shimmering white sheet in the light of the afternoon sun. But immediately after the cliff, the Zuari River widened its mouth to spill its muddy waters into the Arabian Sea. The low hills across the river had not yet been occupied by the Portuguese and were sparsely populated. Paula was in deep concentration, as she deftly transferred the scene onto the paper in front of her. She was totally oblivious of the Captain's presence. He crept up behind her and covered her eyes with his palms.

"Help!" She whispered smiling, for she knew who it was.

"I was thinking . . . Pedro and you have planned this all, haven't you?"

Paula blushed as she turned around. The Captain didn't give her a chance to speak as he kissed her passionately. Then he sat down besides her, near a tree.

"Sorry Lino, I broke my promise . . . but I couldn't bear to see you ignoring me", she told him tenderly, touching his face.

"Don't say sorry, my love. I should thank you that you had the courage to fix this meeting", he told her, bending down to caress her lips with his.

"Fine, next time, it will be your turn to fix a date, and you will see me flying to you", she replied.

The man with his eyelids removed looked like one from hell, with his large eyeballs fully open, almost popping out of their sockets. His tormentors had already begun to dismember him very slowly, beginning with the little finger on his right hand.

"You are an imposter! Parading to be a man of God when in actual fact, you are a criminal wanted in Macau!" screamed the Chief Inquisitor.

"Father please have mercy on me. I am telling you the truth. I am really Padre Ivo", he pleaded.

The hooded executioner brought down his axe in a smooth chopping motion and snipped off the little finger on the other hand. The man screamed in agony and soon fainted with the excruciating pain. He had already lost a lot of blood and life was slowly escaping him.

A helper emptied a bucket of cold water on his face to revive him. They were still not done with him. "*Padre* Simao", called the inquisitor, "come and identify the imposter and criminal".

A priest hobbled inside with the support of a walking stick. It appeared that he did not have a leg.

"It is he for sure, *monsignor*", Padre Simao confirmed. "I saw him taking *Padre* Ivo's bag from the forest, soon after he succumbed to his wounds. I had dragged myself close to where they were after I was mauled by the bear", Padre Simao continued.

"For this and other crimes that you have committed, Repent! We may consider pardoning you", said the Inquisitor.

By now, Ivo had given up hopes of survival. He was convinced that eventually there was going to be no escape for him. The Inquisitors were only trying to prolong his suffering. He had to get this over with quickly. So he scraped up as much spittle as he could and spat in face of the Chief inquisitor, thus angering him greatly.

Enraged, he stood up, stamped the floor, looked at the executioner, made a sweeping motion with his palm drawn across his neck in a cutting motion and turned his back on the condemned saying, "God forgive you for your sins".

The executioner severed Ivo's head with a single swing of his blade.

The Old Panjim Church with the BELL OF THE INQUISITION
Photo by Soumyajit Choudhury

An Old Goan House
Photo by Soumyajit Choudhury

Chapter 12

FOUL PLAY

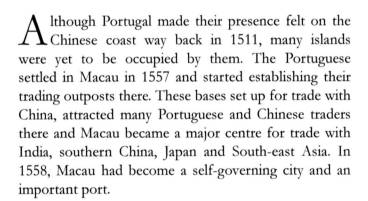

Although Portugal made their presence felt on the Chinese coast way back in 1511, many islands were yet to be occupied by them. The Portuguese settled in Macau in 1557 and started establishing their trading outposts there. These bases set up for trade with China, attracted many Portuguese and Chinese traders there and Macau became a major centre for trade with India, southern China, Japan and South-east Asia. In 1558, Macau had become a self-governing city and an important port.

Lino stared at the command; He had been called to assist against an attack by the Dutch in Macau. Lino's hands trembled, as he read the military mandate to organize the infantry garrison, which was stationed there.

"In appreciation of your exemplary courage under fire and your total dedication to the Crown, His Majesty has decided to give you some well deserved leave. He has personally asked the war office here, to transfer you to Macau for a few months . . ." he read.

Now he was in a dilemma. When he had volunteered for an assignment, he did not imagine that he would be sent out of Goa. Macau came as a shock to him since he didn't want to leave Paula alone with Herodiana for too long a period. Also, he had made all the arrangements to catch her red-handed with her lover; but now if he was going to Macau, he would find it difficult to achieve it.

His thoughts were in a turmoil now. Should he crack the whip at Herodiana now? But then, though he was a successful soldier, he found it difficult to fight social battles. He had to be really angry to barge into her room and tell her that their marriage was null and void. He didn't have any evidence about her lover. About the babies he had documentation, but that was for the Church authorities.

"What should I do now? If I take Paula with me, Herodiana will have an axe to grind. She will draw everyone's sympathy saying that I was always womanizing. She may even say that she aborted the babies because she felt that I would not be a good father . . . . Oh! Lord what should I do now", he muttered to himself, as he paced the floor of his room.

Meanwhile, Herodiana had somehow received news that her husband had met the church authorities. Bufon had also informed her that Lino had gone to see the doctor who had performed the abortions. Now her scheming mind was working overtime. She knew that she had to do something to save her position here. For the first time she realised that she would be literally on the street without the wealth of this family.

"Can I trust Bufon to help?" she wondered, "That oaf is scared of losing his wife's riches too. So I don't think he will support me if he realises that I have nothing".

She pondered over everything and cursed Paula. "It is because of that whore that all this has happened. I am sure she is in love with Lino. I wish I could catch them in bed", she paused and then smiled. An idea seemed to have struck her.

"Preta, go and call Paula", she shouted out at her slave girl who she had commanded to sit outside the door.

"Ok, Madam", came the reply, and Herodiana heard her footsteps, as she ran to carry out her mistress's wishes. Paula was surprised to be summoned by Herodiana. Usually she never did so in the evenings. As she approached the lady's door, she was surprised to see it being opened swiftly.

"Come, my dear. Come on in", said Herodiana. Paula was rooted to the spot for a moment. "Are you shy? Don't worry I will not eat you up, I am keeping the door open, if you are worried", stated Herodiana, pushing the door open.

"Why did you call me, my lady?" asked Paula in a gentle tone.

"Why? Can't I call you, dear?" said Herodiana with a laugh, "I called you to have tea with me today. We haven't chatted for a long time. Tell me how you are keeping".

"Oh! Thank you my lady. That is so kind of you", replied Paula, who was a little suspicious now. The past few years had made her wary of people who spoke too sweetly.

"I really missed you, Paula. Didn't you miss me?" asked Herodiana.

"Well . . . I was busy praying . . ." replied Paula.

"Praying!" exclaimed Herodiana.

"Yes, I had decided to become a nun, but when the Master told me that you were having a tough time without me, I decided to serve you with the same humility", replied Paula, surprised at her own answer.

Herodiana didn't know what to say next. She realised that Paula may have been telling the truth for she knew that the story could be checked as there was only one convent around.

After Paula left, she was fuming again. "Paula, I will get you yet. I may not catch Lino with you. But I will find a way. Even if I have to leave this place, I will not go without dragging you down too", she vowed to herself.

...❦◆❧...

That night Paula had a visitor. She would not have heard the gentle knock on her door, if the strong wind outside hadn't knocked the vase off the table. She awoke with a jolt and listened for signs of others waking with the sound. It was then that she heard the soft knocking at the door.

"Looks like the noise did disturb someone", she said to herself, as she lit a candle, and then tiptoed to the door.

She unlatched the door and looked out in the corridor. But it was dark in there. "Who is it?" She whispered loudly.

"It's me whispered a male voice which she recognized to be the Captain's.

She felt her heart beating so hard that she thought that it might wake up the whole household. She opened the door and let him in.

"It was only a vase" she said nervously, pointing to the floor.

"Calm down my love. Don't worry. Put out the candle", he whispered.

He sat on the bed, near Paula and put his arm around her, holding her close to him. Thus seated, he broke the news of his transfer to her. Neither of them spoke for a long while. They could only feel each other's suffocated breathing and the wetness of their tears as they mingled together. He kissed her passionately and then stood up, for he didn't want to risk getting caught by Herodiana.

"Take care darling, I will be back after a couple of months", he reassured her. "I will still try my best to see you before I go. Maybe we can meet somewhere outside the house".

When Paula woke up the next day, she remembered the Captain's visit and what he had told her. She wept bitterly as she was overcome with fear. She remembered the terrible ordeal at Santa Casa and all that had happened to her after that.

She forced herself to think of the happy times they had together. "Thank you Lord for all that transpired. For the happy times I spent with the Captain after all, was well worth the suffering", she prayed aloud.

Later that morning, Herodiana sent Paula and Preta to the market for the first time.

On her return, Paula got the news that the Captain had been looking out for her. Disappointed at not meeting him, she checked under her pillow. And there, she found a note.

Only two words were written on it: 'Sunset point' and it had the Captain's seal on it.

Sunset point had now become Paula's and Lino's favourite spot. She had decided to go out on her own, since a carriage would attract attention. In any case, Pedro was not around too, because Herodiana had sent him on an errand. She was now confident of finding her way on her own and her excitement to meet her lover had extinguished all her fears.

She hurried to the cliff and waited for him, the shawl wrapped around her neck as usual. It had become one of the most prized possessions in her life. The Captain's first gift!

Suddenly, she heard a noise behind her. Without looking behind, she whispered out his name. "Lino, my love".

But instead of his loving arms encircling her waist, somebody shoved her from behind. She heard laughter, which sounded very evil. She knew who it was, so she relaxed because she didn't expect the person to harm her fatally. However she was wrong as she was shoved harder this time towards the treacherous edge of the cliff. As Paula lost her balance, she tried to grab onto something. But she only managed to clutch an earring of her assailant, tearing it away from her earlobe. With a loud cry to her God, she fell off the edge, into the darkness below.

As she fell, the shawl came loose and slowly descended snakily in the air, only to get snagged on a branch of an overhanging bush, a few yards below the rocky edge. The pain of a torn and bleeding ear was nothing compared to the joy Paula's killer felt over her accomplishment.

...❧◆❧...

Meanwhile, the Captain received fresh orders not to board the ship bound for Macau. He was taken to a 'nau', whose destination was not known even to the captain. On board was a high ranking official who had just arrived from Portugal two months earlier. For the first time, the Captain was concerned about where his new military assignment would take him. He realized that in spite of all his decorations, he was still a puppet.

Lino wished that he had met Paula the day he left home. Instead he had met only Herodiana who appeared to be in a good mood. "I wonder where everyone else was?" he had asked himself, as he realised that even his trusted valet Pedro was not around.

"Oh Lord, I hope Herodiana was not up to some mischief!" he exclaimed. He had heard that Preta was out with Paula too. He knew that his wife never sent the poor slave girl anywhere.

Just then his thoughts were interrupted by a troop of men who came to him and saluted. "Reporting for duty under your command, Sir!" they said. He noticed that all of them were new to him. Not a single one was from his old command. In fact they were all wearing a new type of uniform. "What type of exercise is this?" he wondered.

...❧◆❧...

On the island of Madagascar, the white-furred ring-tailed *'maki'* (lemur in Malagasy), seated high above a tall baobab tree, had its eyes transfixed on the burial ground of the Merina tribe. There was a gathering of about twenty men, both young and old, chanting around what appeared to be an exhumed body that lay beside a freshly dug grave.

The rite of *'famidihana'* was not uncommon within the Merino and Betsileo tribes of Madagascar. It involved the reburial or 'turning over' of the dead. In this ritual, the relative's remains were removed from the grave and rewrapped in new silk shrouds and returned to the grave, following festive ceremonies in their honour. They believed that the dead joined their ancestors in the ranks of divinity and that the ancestors are intensely concerned with the fate of their living descendents.

The Malagasy people had arrived on the island of Madagascar around 2000 years ago, after traveling an astounding 4000 miles from the Indonesian archipelago in simple outrigger canoes. Ever since, they had reared cattle and goats and hunted native animals for food.

Suddenly, the gathering below was disturbed by the loud bang of a musket going off and out of the didiera thorn bush, rushed a wild pig apparently wounded by a hunter. Soon, a towering black man stepped out of the bushes looking for his prey. He was a member of the pirate settlement at the northern end of the island, most hated by the Merinos. Ever since the Pirates had occupied the Bay which stretched from Mahajanga to Antsiranana, indigenes of the island had taken a hatred to the foreigners. Also, the arrival of Portuguese missionaries had made relations even worse, as they tried in vain to convert them to Christianity. This hatred was evident from the manner in which the young men from the Merino tribe attacked the hunter. Deciding to make an example out of him, the elders ordered him to be hung from a tamarind tree as a warning to others not to trespass on their sacred land.

"Captain", said the Commander of the secret operation. "Soon, we will be approaching the island of Madagascar from the north-eastern side. Your mission is to land on the beach with your select men and cross over to the other side, to the Bay of Mahajanga where you will have to take the enemy by surprise. Remember, that there may be women and children there and they must not be harmed. Try to catch Sergio and Algernon alive for the king, if possible. Let us avoid bloodshed at any cost".

Inwardly, Lino was very happy that he was going there. Now that he knew that Clara was captive on the island, he wished to free her from the pirates and bring her back to Goa.

"I will do it for Paula", he thought, imagining the happy reunion between the two.

The Captain of the 'Santa Luiza' was an old and experienced seadog who knew those waters well. He expertly maneuvered the vessel away from the treacherous reefs and dropped anchor in a sheltered bay. The small boats were loaded with ammunition that was enough to breach a hole in the strongest of barricades. About the fifty well trained men pulled strongly at the oars of their small boats and within no time, reached the beach. As they headed for the island they noticed smoke rising up through the trees. It was definitely too much to be from chimneys and too little to be a forest fire. They unloaded the boats quickly and moored them under a rocky overhang, out of site from any scouts who may have been placed at the top of the cliff. Spreading out in two packs of twenty-five each, with Lino leading one of the packs, they made their own path through the dense outgrowth with their swords. The lemurs and the parrots made a right din and they hoped that they wouldn't be discovered. After crossing the forest of large balboas they suddenly reached a clearing which brought them almost to the edge of a cliff. Lying low, Captain ordered his men to be quiet while they waited for the others to join them. In the meanwhile, Lino crawled to the edge of the cliff and looked down below. To his horror, he saw at least 50 small houses reduced to cinders and further beyond in the bay, a large sailing ship and smaller vessels were all burning rapidly, aided by the fanning from the breeze. There seemed to have been some kind of an attack. The whole place lay still. The ground appeared to be littered with dead and injured bodies.

"It looks like the pirates have been taken unawares by some attackers", said Lino, "We must proceed post-haste to the settlement below and tend to the wounded if any".

By this time the second group of men had already arrived and joined the descent to the settlement below. It was truly a gory sight with bodies scattered all over. It appeared that the pirates had been totally taken by surprise! Some of the men were still in their undergarments.

"Attend to the wounded and look around for the women and children. They must have found refuge in the surrounding caves on the hillside", shouted the Captain.

It did not take them long to find the women who had in fact done just as the Captain had thought . . . At least twenty women had holed up in the inner recesses of a cave that was well hidden in a cluster of tall brush. They were all African.

"Where is Clara?" He wondered as he scanned each face. But there was no sign of a fair-skinned maiden anywhere.

"Captain, Captain . . . . Over here". There was a shout from behind what appeared to be the remains of a store of some sort. The Captain hurried over and was caught totally off guard, as he saw an attractive woman of about eighteen years of age cradling the head of a white man who appeared to be struggling for life. There was with a crude spear protruding from his chest. Beside him lay another white man, with his head almost severed from his body.

"Clara?" Lino whispered softly. I am Captain Lino of the infantry regiment from the City of Goa. I have come to take you to safety"

"I was safe here with my beloved Sergio until . . . .the . . . the natives attacked suddenly and we were all caught unawares. My Sergio fought valiantly but we were all badly outnumbered. He may have been a pirate to Portugal but he was a good man and everyone here adored him", she sobbed.

"Paula thought you were dead until she saw your shell necklace on a slave girl from the Comoros islands"

"Paula? And how do you know her?" she asked, forgetting her grief for a moment.

"She must have mentioned to you about where she was going to work". He replied

"You are Captain Abranches, aren't you?" she exclaimed.

"Yes, I am he", he said smiling warmly.

CHAPTER 13

THE DIARY

In the early light of Dawn, everybody in Oddavel was still fast asleep. All the tiny huts scattered at intervals amongst the coconut palms of the Abranches grove, were dark silhouettes against the sky. But Kistu, the toddy-tapper was an early riser. Today he had to go down to the grove close to the rocks below the cliff. He was whistling a tune, as he picked up a sickle from the hook which was hung next to the kitchen door. His dear wife was already up and making breakfast for him.

They were a happy couple with two sons. Lately they had more cause for joy, because their little son, who was always very sick, was perfectly fine now. Kistu bent down and kissed him as he slept soundly on a mat in their small room.

"God bless Dona Paula", he whispered, as he remembered the lady who worked for his master. She was the one who had personally taken his *morgado* (beloved) to a good

European doctor in the City of Goa. "Such a kindly soul", he thought.

In fact, the whole of Oddavel had been sad when she had gone missing. And to express their love, they had given her a floral welcome, when she had visited the village, just a week back.

As Kistu, walked along the shore, he saw some seagulls circling the rocks making a lot of noise. He wondered what had disturbed them. But the toddy-tapper knew that no one ventured out so early in the morning. Robbers were out of question because the Portuguese laws were very strict. No one would dare touch somebody else's belongings. It was so safe that people did not bother to even lock their doors.

"Wonder why they are so agitated", he said to himself, as he started jogging towards the spot. As he neared the rocks, he saw someone lying on them. "I wonder who that is?" he said to himself. His heart was pounding hard as he drew closer to the body. He could see that whoever it was, she had been dead a long time ago. A lump formed in his throat as he overturned the body. "Paula", he gasped and ran all the way back crying hysterically. People came out of their houses and soon a big crowd gathered. The women started sobbing when the toddy-tapper described what he had seen for everyone loved the sweet and gentle lady from Portugal.

Word was sent to Pedro who had gone to his cousin's place on the island of Divar for the village feast. By the time the body of Paula was brought to the *cuartel* (police station), Pedro and Ana had returned. Both were crying bitterly.

"What happened? Where was she found?" the old valet asked the crowd. Kistu stepped forward and explained to him how he had found her on the rocks. Pedro closed his eyes as the tears welled up.

He fought back all sorts of thoughts. "No! Paula was a God-fearing person . . . she would never commit suicide", he said to himself. The police had decided that it was a suicide and had sent word to the branches to collect the body.

Pedro and Ana escorted the body of the woman who had brought so much joy to his wife and him. Preta was sobbing bitterly, as the body was laid in the hall, on a well decorated table that was being used by the house staff as their dining table.

Herodiana broke the silence with her sobs, as she came down from her room. "Oh Paula, why did you have to end your life like this?" she cried.

Her words made Pedro's blood boil, but he controlled himself. He left the room to make the necessary arrangements. The man he had sent to the army headquarters had returned to say that the master had left on a secret mission.

All the people who knew her were steeped in mourning over the death of this wonderful lady. Everyone believed it to be a suicide but no one could find the motive.

The funeral was well attended. Almost the whole village of Oddavel was there to pay their last respects to an honourable lady.

The officers apologized to Lino for the secrecy. It had been a sad but successful operation that was held at Madagascar. Although there was hardly any fighting, Lino was not happy with the way it turned out since the natives had massacred all the pirates and their families. Clara had convinced him that they were not pirates if viewed from the right perspective. Lino was already against slavery long before this happened but he could not take a stance against it because of its wide acceptance in all their lands. All he could do was to at least change the things in his own household. For a start, he decided to free the slaves attached to his household.

Clara was very quiet throughout the journey back to Goa. She was still heartbroken over the loss of her beloved Sergio. Only one thought consoled her and that was the knowledge that Paula would be there for her.

The few who met him at the dock greeted him in a somber manner. Linda, who had come with Theresa to meet Clara at the dock, were the only ones who were overjoyed at seeing Clara after such a long separation. Lino was too busy with his thoughts to notice their behaviour. None of the officers wanted to break the news to him about Paula, as they were still in shock over the tragedy. By now they had guessed that the Captain loved her very much. In fact they had been happy about it, as they knew how much he had suffered after marrying Herodiana.

Herodiana was in her balcony reflecting on the turn of events, when she heard Lino's voice coming from downstairs. Padre Ivo's capture by the inquisition had come as a big blow to her but on the other hand, she had to keep her head around more immediate matters in the house now. She hurriedly changed into her mourning attire cursing, "Macau . . . that liar. I have to warn Bufon now. My plans are all *merde*", she grumbled.

Preta was very angry to see her mistress play-acting again. She had seen the master entering too. Herodiana brushed past her and went downstairs, crying out loudly, "Oh Lino, our Paula is no more. Our Paula is no more. She has ended her sweet life".

Lino couldn't believe his ears. He moved away from Herodiana's embrace and went past her to look for Pedro. The old man was sitting on a stone seat outside the kitchen. He looked haggard and disheveled. His hair was tousled and his eyes had huge dark rings around them. He seemed to be totally unaware of the Master's presence.

"Pedro . . . Pedro. It is me Lino", he declared, pumping his arm gently.

But the old man just stared at the floor, expressionless. "Pedro, please tell me. Where is Paula? Someone please say something", he cried, feeling the tears rolling down his cheeks, as he shook the old man. Pedro stood up and embraced his Master.

"Master", he wept, "Dear Paula is no more".

The Captain didn't know what was happening to him, as he found himself in a daze. When he regained his composure he once again wanted to know what had happened. Choking on his own words, Pedro haltingly told him everything that had happened.

"Please Lino, tell me. Do you believe it is suicide? Did Paula end her life?" pleaded the Captain.

"No Master I don't believe it. But it does appear so", said Pedro in a choking tone.

...❧◆❧...

It had been two days, since Paula had been done to death. Though he was tired and in shock, the Captain insisted on going to Oddavel. Pedro tried to hold him back but he wouldn't listen. So finally the old man decided to escort him.

Pedro took off to Kistu's house with his master straightaway. The toddy-tapper was at home. He had not been keeping well since the day he had spotted Paula's body.

"Tell the master all that you told me when you found the Lady", Pedro instructed him.

In a tearful tone, Kistu told him everything that had to be told. The Captain grimaced when he described the injuries. The toddy-tapper than agreed to escort them to the spot. The Captain looked all around the rocks. Then he looked up at the overhanging cliff. Suddenly his body tensed. His sharp eyes had picked up something.

He pointed it out to Pedro. It was a piece of cloth that seemed to be fluttering in the breeze on a shrub close to the edge. They then ran to their horses and rode up to 'sunset point'. They scanned the place meticulously for any other clues besides the piece of cloth they had seen from the rocks below. The ever-alert military officer located the shawl. Hooking it off the shrub with a long twig, he cried as he held it. It had a large "P" embroidered on it. It was the same shawl, which he had gifted Paula, after he had spoken to her on this very hill. "It started here and ended here". He couldn't control himself thinking that way, as he sat on the ground feeling weak in the knees.

As he stared at the ground in sorrow, he saw something glinting in the rays of the setting sun. He picked it and gaped at it in horror. It was an earring, which he recognized at once. At that moment, he remembered the wound that he had noticed on Herodiana's right ear, which she was trying very hard to conceal with her hair, when he had entered the house that morning.

Pedro watched his master, not understanding his master's reaction. Lino checked his pistol as he mounted his steed in a flying jump. He looked furious, as he tore down the hill. The Captain was right about the identity of the murderer. It was Herodiana who had taken the opportunity to do away with the girl who had upset all her plans!

Herodiana heard that the Captain had received a transfer notice and kept a watch on him. That whole night she pretended to be asleep as she had guessed that he would make his way to Paula's room. Standing outside, she heard the whole conversation.

The next morning, she purposely sent Paula to the market. And it paid off, for when the Captain came home, he didn't find her. So as soon as her husband left, Herodiana hurried to Paula's room and groped under her pillow. There she found a note which read:

"My love, I have to leave now—will not be able to see you today—Cannot wait till I get back—love you" It was signed Lino.

She tore the note in anger and spat on it. Then she crept into her husband's room and forged a note in her husband's handwriting. She stamped it with the Captain's personal seal and then kept it under Paula's pillow.

Herodiana knew about Sunset Point because the Captain used to take her there often, soon after their marriage. However, life at the Abranches household was very slow and boring for her. Besides, she hardly had any interest in nature and abhorred spending time with Lino as they always argued about having a child.

...❧◆❧...

Herodiana was on the balcony when Lino stormed into the front yard. She seemed to be watching him as he looked up. Lino wanted to yell at her from below, but he controlled his anger. He kicked the front door open, and ran up the steps, taking them two at a time.

With a powerful kick, he broke the door of his wife's room and stormed into the balcony. But his dramatic entry seemed to have no effect on Herodiana. She seemed to be in some kind of a drunken stupor, her head buried into her folded hands resting on the railing. A broken wineglass littered the floor.

This inebriated surrounding and his wife's lack of reaction further infuriated the Captain, who drew his loaded pistol and put his gun to her head shouting, "You dirty killer, I will see that you will meet the same end as . . ."

He stopped in mid-sentence, as he felt her to be cold to his touch as he yanked her back. He staggered back in horror. And Herodiana fell to the floor lifeless. She had been dead for a while!

The Captain didn't believe it to be suicide, as he knew that Herodiana was a woman who loved her life over everything else.

...❧◆❧...

The police had hardly started on Paula's case and now it was Herodiana. Captain was in a real fix giving hundreds of statements, signing papers and of course arranging the funeral for Herodiana. Whilst the body was still at the morgue for a proper autopsy, Lino had a little respite until the trial and verdict. He had no qualms about being cleared of any criminal suspicion over both Paula's and Herodiana's death. It would be some time before the actual trial would get underway.

Meanwhile, the next evening, Lino visited the cliff again. His heart was in turmoil. How much he had longed to meet Paula. He had decided to end his long defunct marriage with Herodiana. But now all was lost.

'Sunset Point'. The name that he had given this spot now held a new significance for him. Now the sun had indeed set on his life at this very place, that they both had loved so much.

He sat there looking seawards at the setting sun. He then closed his eyes as he felt the closeness of Paula. Suddenly he was disturbed by a soft whimpering sound. At first he ignored it thinking it to be a puppy. But when he heard it again, he realised that it came from the edge of the cliff.

He stood up and walked to the spot, and when he looked over the edge, he was shocked to see their slave-girl Preta. She was caught in the same bush, where he had found Paula's shawl.

...᳆✦᳆...

Runaway slaves once caught could get subjected to rape and molestation by their finders, since the original masters could not be there to protect them. Preta knew this fact and realized that it would not be long before someone spotted her and reported her to the police. She also knew that by this time the doctors may have found out that Herodiana was poisoned.

She remembered the person who had meant everything to her. The only person who had shown her love, Paula! With Paula gone, she decided to end her life. She had even decided on the spot. So she climbed up to the top of the cliff in Oddavel, the very same the hillock where her dear Paula usually went to do her paintings. Paula had herself pointed it out to the slave-girl.

Standing at the edge of the cliff, she closed her eyes and stepped off the rock on which she was standing. As she fell, a bush growing at the edge broke her fall and the dry twigs tore into her dress and held onto her. She had looked down and panic made her change her decision to end her life!

As Preta lay on the branch, terrified at the prospect of falling off it, suddenly she heard a gasp and a voice call out her name. She immediately recognized the voice of the Captain. After tying a rope to a tree trunk, the Captain lowered himself down to where Preta was snagged and tied the rope around her slender waist. Soon he was up and over the cliff and pulling away at the rope. Preta, helped relieve the weight by trying to put her feet on some protruding rocks. As soon as she was out of danger, she fell at his feet and apologised. Then in a trembling voice, she told him everything that had happened.

She had overheard Herodiana talking to her lover Amorous discussing her plan to get rid of Paula. But the latter had declined to carry out the plot. She had shouted at him and threatened to end their relationship but still he had refused. Then the day the Captain had left on his secret mission, Preta had seen her enter his room and then followed her down to Paula's room. She had seen her tearing a note and then writing another one. Of course she didn't understand what her mistress was doing.

But when the Captain heard it, he knew that Herodiana must have switched the notes.

"But why didn't you warn Paula?" he asked the slave-girl.

Preta started sobbed incessantly. "It was too late . . . Master, Senhora had already left the house. Senhor Pedro go to market. Oh . . . Dona Paula love me much", she sobbed in despair.

"She always tell me . . . master solve my problem . . . she speak to you. But then . . ." she revealed, breaking in mid-sentence, as sobs racked her chest.

The Captain was listening intently, tears filling up his eyes, as he thought of Paula and how much everybody loved her.

Preta had been heartbroken when she saw Paula's lifeless body. She had been further angered by the pretense that

Herodiana had been putting up, when the body was being brought in.

"That time, I sure that mistress murder Dona Paula. I see torn ear", she explained between sobs. "I decide I kill her".

She then explained how she had poisoned her with a poisonous herb that she knew of from Africa. Preta then fell at Lino's feet. "Master please kill me. I go where Paula go. I know there, I have freedom", she pleaded of him.

"Preta, go back home as if nothing has happened. You will live in my villa as a free woman. I will draw up the documents later", the Captain told her sadly after a long silence.

Pedro was very concerned about his master. He appeared to have aged considerably in the last few days. He didn't eat properly and every time the old valet told him that he should eat, he replied, "Do you want to extend my pain, Pedro?"

This brought tears to the old man's eyes. He couldn't bear to see his dynamic master in this state. But what could he do. Was there any hope he could offer the Captain? Even he was growing tired of life. After his daughter's death, both Ana and he had found so much consolation in loving Paula. Now life seemed to have suddenly lost its charm for both of them.

A month had passed since Paula had been murdered. By then, Lino was cleared of all suspicion related to the two deaths. Pedro felt that it was time he reminded the master to write to Paula's mother in Portugal. So he went to Lino's room to tell him.

"Thank you Pedro my good man. I know I have been irresponsible. Thank you for reminding me. God bless you", he replied.

"God bless you too, master", said Pedro and as he was about to leave the room, the captain stopped him. "Wait a minute Pedro. I would like you and Ana to pack Paula's belongings. We will have them sent to Portugal", he told Pedro, "I will join you later".

Later, as he watched Pedro and Ana sort through his sweetheart's meager belongings, He struggled to hold back his tears. As Ana was arranging her suitcase, she noticed a secret pouch in the lining of the suitcase. Excitedly, she opened it and pulled out a leather bound diary.

"Please, can you give that to me?" Lino asked politely. He accepted the diary from Ana and took it to his study. With trembling hands, he opened the first page. But he closed it again guiltily and started playing with the red ribbon, book-marking Paula's last entry in the book. Inadvertently he opened it. And what caught his eyes, hit him like a ton of bricks. For written there were the words, "I AM WITH CHILD'. The despair was obvious as she had laid the nib with such force that it had ripped several pages beneath.

His heart now beating rapidly, the Captain, hurriedly read every entry in the book and searched for more references to the child, but in vain.

Whose child? What happened to the child? Where is the child? Such thoughts now filled his mind. He explored every possibility of reconstructing the story. Being human, the thought of another man in Paula's life did crop up but he fought it down, telling himself that Paula was too well bred and dignified to indulge in immoral liaisons. That's when he remembered the passionate night in the quarry.

"So the child must be mine!" He almost screamed thumping the desk with his fist as hope entered his heart again. But first, he had to find the child, he thought. Now Lino felt that there was something to live for—the living symbol of their love.

He tried to focus on all the events of the past after he had rescued her from the Inquisitors. Paula had disappeared from the McKennas'. After that, Lino had arranged a search party throughout the woods. A fisherman had found his canoe missing which had been recovered by other fishermen from the high seas, with his overcoat snagged in the nets on which she must have laid her head.

As these events floated into his consciousness, he suddenly stopped and blurted out, "I have to find the fishermen who found that boat".

He ran down the steps to Pedro's room. He had decided to confide in this man who had been with him, through thick and thin. The old man's eyes filled with tears when Lino told him about the entry in the diary.

Suddenly, hope filled their hearts again. Life had a new meaning again for them. Pedro was doubly happy because now his master had a new hope.

For three days, Lino and Pedro frantically searched for the man whose boat had gone missing. Finally, after many enquiries around the place, they were directed to a small village near the River Mandovi.

As they rode there one morning, they passed close to the McKenna's home. So Lino decided to make a brief stop there.

"Lino . . . so nice to see you", said Greg, who was growing some new plants in his garden. His greeting was so full of life as usual. He gave the captain a bear hug.

"I am so sorry about what happened, Lino", he said. Sabita and He had attended both the funerals.

A voice from within made him confide in Greg and Sabita, although he was embarrassed about it. He told them how much he loved Paula, the babies that Herodiana had killed, the murder and the entry in Paula's diary.

"I want to find that child! That's all I am living for", he told them, sobbing like a little boy.

"Wait a second. Now I know why Paula was not eating properly when she was here", remarked Sabita, "I think she used to get bouts of morning sickness. I remember seeing her bring up a couple of times".

"Maybe she knew that she was pregnant, so she wanted to disappear to save you from social embarrassment", added Greg.

The Captain was filled with remorse. "Oh Paula! Why didn't you tell me? Why did you bear it all alone? Oh! My brave darling!" He went on, bursting into tears.

"Easy Lino, now you have to concentrate on finding the child Paula so bravely brought into this world. For I am sure she is out there somewhere".

After what proved to be an enlightening stop at the McKenna's, Lino and Pedro rode down to the small village near the River Mandovi. There they met Camilo the fisherman. At first he didn't recognize the Captain. Then after Pedro had explained to him, he remembered the gentleman as the one who had come to enquire about the young lady who was missing.

"Please, can you tell us who found your boat?" Pedro questioned him.

"Some fishermen from my old village", he informed him.

After getting their names, Lino and Pedro went to Camilo's old village, where they found the two fishermen, Joaquim and Carmo.

The fishing boat was small and had a stench of fish. The two fishermen, rowed out to sea with their two passengers, always keeping sight of the land. After a long sojourn along the coast to the north of Goa, they stopped rowing and explained that they had found the empty canoe bobbing right where they were.

Lino noted that the spot was close to a deserted beach with a lonely white cross. When he stared at the place, he heard an inner voice beckoning him there. He requested Pedro to ask the fishermen what the place was called. They identified it to be the Morjim beach.

"There is a small fishing village a couple of kilometers from the beach", said Carmo.

Reading Lino's mind, Pedro then requested them to drop them off at the beach.

"Don't worry, we will find our way back", Pedro said to them. Lino offered them some money but they refused to accept it and deftly turned the boat around and headed home.

The first thing that Lino and Pedro did was to go to the whitewashed cross and pray for God's guidance in solving this mystery. They followed the well-worn footpath in the fading light as the sun dipped its orange face below the horizon.

After a few kilometers of walking in silence, each man lost in his own thoughts, came upon the village. There was a lot of activity around as the men were getting ready to go fishing that evening.

Pedro tried to fish out some information about Paula, but to no avail. As they approach the centre of the village they heard someone call out to them in Portuguese.

When they turned around, they saw an elderly man, standing outside a cozy little cottage. "Gentlemen, *por favore*. Let's talk", said Isidore.

Pedro looked at Lino, who nodded his approval.

"Isidore introduced himself and his wife who was standing in the doorway of the cottage.

"Isidore, why don't you call them inside?" Suggested the ever intuitive Bella.

"Gentlemen, please come in", he told them, shaking their hands and then leading them in, "I heard that you were enquiring about Paula".

"Ye . . . Ye . . . Yes! We wanted to know about Paula. Why? Do you know her? Ple . . . ease tell me", said the Captain eagerly.

"But pray, may I know who you are?" asked Isidore.

"Oh! Sorry. I am Lino and, this is my good friend Pedro", said Lino apologetically.

"Lino! At last we meet the man Paula loved so much", said the old man, obviously excited. The old woman too was very elated and she immediately asked about Paula.

Both the Captain and Pedro were silent.

"Why are you quiet? Is everything okay with Paula? The last time I saw her, my child was very crestfallen and looked so much like a nun in her habit!" Isidore exclaimed in a concerned voice.

"She is no longer in this world. She left us last month". Pedro told them softly.

On hearing this news, Bella fainted. The old man was too shocked to even attend to her.

After placing Bella on a mat and reviving her with cool water from the well, the Captain who saw them so emotionally affected, felt compelled to tell them the whole story.

He told them of how he had met Paula, the rescue from the Inquisitors, her disappearance, the chance meeting at the Convent, their reconciliation and her return to the Abranches household, and lastly her murder on the cliff by his own unfaithful wife.

They were clearly heartbroken. But Isidore found his voice. "Son, Paula became the daughter we didn't have. And though, she stayed with us for a short while, it was a lifetime for us", he declared with tears in his eyes. Then he told them about how the child was born, the smallpox epidemic and how he had introduced to Sr.Magdalena.

"I wanted to see her so much, but then I fell sick and was unable to travel", he added, wiping the tears which filled his eyes.

"I hope you find Paulina. I am sure Sr. Magdalena will help you", said Isidore.

Lino gave Isidore and Bella a warm hug and said, "Thank you for all that you did for Paula.

"She was our *namorada* too", said Bella, "It was our pleasure to have her with us".

Lino and Pedro then travelled back on a bullock cart that was carrying hay for the military stables in the City of Goa. They reached the mansion late in the evening. The next morning Pedro went to the Royal Convent of Santa Monica to leave a message for Sister Magdalena that Lino would like to see her.

Chapter14

ILLEGAL ADOPTION

When the news about Paula's tragic death reached her, Sr. Magdalena had been heartbroken and had fallen ill. She then vowed to make Paula's dreams come true. Paula had always spoken about taking her child away from Goa and send the baby to her mother in Portugal.

But when she visited the *Recolhimento de Nossa Senhora de Serra,* she was shocked to find out that the child had already been given up for adoption. She approached the Regente, who had newly joined there.

"How could you do such a thing?" Sr. Magdalena had shouted in anger, losing her composure for the first time.

When she approached the *'Provedor'* who happened to be in the house, she realised that he was hand in glove with the *Regente.* In fact the *'Porteira',* a kindhearted lady, later informed Sister Magdalena that the couple who adopted the baby was childless and were going back to Portugal.

They had offered the Provedor and Regente a large sum of money. Also, the new Regente didn't like the idea of looking after a baby that small.

"I will go to the *Mesa*, and tell them what you did" she had said to the Provedor.

"Madre, I know that you are a person who keeps your word. I am sure you won't like the father of Paula's child to know about his secret child?"

Sr. Magdalena was shell-shocked that somehow, these persons had found out even that.

"God will punish you evil ones", she had told them and stormed out of the *Recolhimento*.

Now Sr. Magdalena was deep in thought, when she was told that Lino was already waiting for her. As she headed for the parlour, a thought struck her, "Could Lino have been the father of the child?"

When she saw the Captain, she was taken aback. He looked very haggard and looked half the size she first saw him. He seemed to have lost all zest for life.

"My son, what has happened to you? You look completely defeated", she said to him tenderly.

Lino was touched by the concern in her voice. "Sister, please forgive me. But after the death of Paula I have never been the same. I loved her, Madre. Yes Madre, I loved her dearly", he lamented.

"Calm down, my child. Tell me if there is anyway I can help you with", she said.

"Help me get my child back. It is only for this fruit of our love that I live. I wish Paula had confessed to me everything", he said adding, "Maybe I deserved this punishment because I was the cause of all that happened to Paula". He told Sister about all that had happened in his life. About Herodiana and how she treated Paula. "She never complained. She was indeed an angel. My dear Paula".

It was exactly like how Sr. Magdalena had envisaged however, now she was not sure whether to tell him everything about the child.

With tears in her eyes, Sister Magdalena said, "Yes, Paula was an angel indeed. She always wanted to protect your name".

"Sister, do you know about the child?" he asked softly.

"Ye . . . Ye . . . Yes", she stammered, pausing to catch her breath, "I am sorry that I didn't mention it. But please don't misunderstand me. I didn't know that you were the father", said Sr. Magdalena. "She also told me about little Paulina and her plans to take the baby back to Portugal".

Tears ran down Lino's cheeks as he listened to Sister Magdalena.

"But where is the child now?" he interrupted impatiently, rising to his feet, wide eyed.

Now it was Sr. Magdalena's turn to cry. In between sobs, she told him about keeping the child at the *Recolhimento* and about the adoption

Lino slumped back into his seat. He put his head between his hands in disbelief.

...ॐ♦ॐ...

The next day saw the Captain at the *Recolhimento de Nossa Senhora de Serra.*

"I have come for the child of Paula", Lino told the *Regente.*

"But we don't have any such child", said the Regente.

"Sr. Magdalena will testify about that. She told me that you gave her up for adoption. I think that was against the rule. I will report to . . ."

"That Sr. Magdalena", muttered the *Regente"*. But Wait . . . I will see that the father of the child knows this little secret . . ."

"What secret?" interrupted Lino, "Who are you threatening? You can't use that threat against me".

"I am sure Sr. Magdalena wouldn't like to give away the secrets of a dead waif".

"Waif! How dare you call Paula a waif? She was an angel".

"Angel", scoffed the *Regente*.

"My lady, please stop insulting Paula. I am not here to argue. I just want to know the name and address of the people who adopted Paulina".

"That is against our rules. I cannot give you the names".

"But isn't giving away the baby for adoption without the prior consent of the parent, also against the Rules?"

"That is none of your business", said the *Regente*, who was not used to anyone speaking back to her.

"I am going to the *Mesa* to complain to them about this adoption".

"And who are you to carry out such an investigation?" Asked the Regente, visibly angered at the threat.

"I am the father of the child!" Burst out Lino.

These words startled the *Regente*, who almost fell off her chair. She had now lost all her bravado and shifted uncomfortably in her seat. "My Lord, I will give you all the information you want", she said with a sudden change in attitude.

"Then hand over all the documents regarding the child", said the Captain.

"Sorry, but I gave them to the couple who adopted the child". Said the Regente fearfully.

"But you will have some carbon copies made in your book?" yelled the annoyed Lino.

The *Regente* called for the *Porteira* and asked her to get the registration book which contained the records of all the children brought up at the *Recolhimento*, given up for adoption, etc. Then copying down the details, she handed them over to Lino. She also wrote down the address of the party who had adopted the child—Henri Almeida.

Lino took the paper from the *Regente* and studied them. Suddenly he looked up, "But this address is in Goa".

"Yes, they are living in Goa".

Lino gave her a hard look, and then realized that the lady was telling the truth.

…❧♦❧…

"Henri Almeida has sold his estate in Goa and has gone back to Portugal", the *escrivao* at the Viceroy's Office informed Lino.

"Can you give me his address in Portugal?"

"My Lord, Henri Almeida is the Conde de Almeida and you will find him at the Almeida Castle on the outskirts of Lisboa", replied the *escrivao* after going through some documents.

"Has he left Goa?" asked Lino impatiently.

"Yes, Sir, according to this permit signed by the Viceroy, he left along with his family, two months ago".

"The whole Family?"

"Yes three of them . . . The *Conde*, his wife and their little daughter".

...꒰♦꒱...

When Amorous Bufon got the news about Herodiana's death, he was sick with rage but not in the least grieved. He was not exactly grieved; At least not like a man who had lost his lover but more like a dog that had lost his bone. He now had to find someone who could match her sexual prowess.

"Lino, I will get you for this. I will finish you off very slowly", he declared loudly.

His chances of getting his hands on the Abranches estate were now gone. Now he had to do what he always feared. He had to give up his palatial mansion, because he could no longer maintain it. Soon after marriage he had given up his job as a military adviser, mainly because he was a coward and was fearful of coming under fire. He had squandered away the wealth of the family. The only way he could sponsor his wife's social life, was through the money he got from Herodiana who stole and sold the Abranches family jewels.

Amorous had to put aside his thoughts as he saw his wife enter the room.

"Aha, darling, I was just coming to meet you. I have received mail from Portugal. My cousin who looked after the Almeida Castle in Lisboa has died and I have been asked to take charge of it now. I will have to go to Portugal urgently", he announced, taking her in his arms.

She kissed him on his cheek and sat on his lap.

"Darling I can't leave you here. I can't live without you", he said to her coyly. Surprisingly, it had its effect on his wife.

"Of course I will come too. But Henri, I want a child".

"Come we will make one . . ."

"Stop that vulgar talk Henri. You know very well that I can never have one".

He laughed. "Well then, what child are you talking about?"

"We will adopt one. We have to do that because I can't face my cousins in Portugal. They will mock me. Besides I have already told them a lie about having a daughter".

"Then what do you intend doing?"

"Well I have already spoken to the *Regente* at the *Recolhimento de Nossa Senhora de Serra*. She has a pretty little girl with them. She is around three years old", she stated.

"So you have been searching?" he asked of her.

"Yes, I have darling. So come, we will go and adopt her".

"But what about her parentage? She may have been born out of mixed marriage", he said trying to discourage her because he didn't like the idea of looking after a child.

"Tomorrow we will go there and find out", she said to Amorous firmly. He just nodded his head, because he didn't want to irritate her. After all, her wealth in Portugal would surely come in handy.

But little did Amarella know that he had decided to go to the *Recolhimento* without her.

...❧◆☙...

"Dona Fransquina, I think my wife approached you for the adoption of a child", he said to the Regente.

"Hush, not so loudly. Come into my office. We will discuss the matter there".

She ushered Amorous into her little office.

"We have decided not to take a child without being sure about her parentage. She may belong to some '*caçado*'.

"No, no. She does not have mixed blood in her", smiled the Regente.

"But what makes you so sure about that?"

"Well, I will tell you. But it is a secret which you have to keep", she told him, lowering her voice further.

"Then tell me quickly".

"Yes, the mother is a lady named Paula who came here with Sr. Magdalena from the Convent of Santa Monica".

Amorous Bufon almost choked. He was obviously delighted.

"Ha, Ha, Paula had an illegitimate child", he muttered to himself and then turning to the Regente he said, "Tell me about the father. What about the father?"

"Well, according to Dona Alcina, the nurse who often goes to the Convent to treat the nuns, one day she was asked to treat Paula. She had fever and was delirious and kept muttering a man's name", she told him.

"Tell me . . . tell me. What was the name she muttered?" Bufon asked her anxiously.

The Regente gave him a look. "Why are you so interested? Do you know them, Sir?"

"Never mind that, ma'am. Can you tell me the name please?"

"Lino". That's the name she kept on muttering. I put two and two together and arrived to the conclusion that Lino is the father of the child", she revealed pompously, thrilled at her little deduction.

Amorous simply couldn't believe what he had stumbled on. "Now I know what lesson I will teach Lino", he whispered to himself.

...❧✦❧...

"Darling, I have a gift for you to take to Portugal".

Lady Amarella came running into the parlour and was startled to hear a little child's voice.

"Hello mama", she said.

Amorous had taught the friendly little girl what to say, promising to take her on a ride on a big ship. When Lady Amarella drew near, the little girl stepped out from behind Amorous and ran towards her.

"What a lovely child. Everyone in Portugal will admire her", she said, brushing the girl's hair. She was more concerned about the impression she would have on her friends in Portugal.

She too had actually never been really interested in a child after the doctor told her that she would be unable to conceive. Lady Amarella was also an epileptic, and that was what upset Amorous very much. He tolerated her only because of her wealth.

Lino and Pedro visited the Conde d'Almeida's mansion. It had been put up for sale.

"Perhaps I will find some clues here", he said to himself.

When he entered, one of the caretakers, an old man of around 70, greeted Pedro.

"Hello Caetano, how are you?" Pedro replied, "You must be missing the Conde".

"No, no, Pedro. Not the young one if you mean him. "But the old man, surely, I miss him", he said.

Whilst Pedro and Caetano chatted in the kitchen, Lino asked permission to explore the many rooms of the castle. As he roamed around aimlessly, he came across a wing which was hardly furnished.

"This must be the old wing", he said to himself. Suddenly, he saw what appeared to be drops of blood on the floor. These appeared to have dried up.

The Captain followed the trail and to his surprise it ended near a blank wall. He got onto his hands and knees and to his surprise saw one of the drops was partly under the wall!

At that moment he heard Pedro calling out to him.

He stood up and called out to him, "I am here, Pedro. Come on up", he shouted out.

To his surprise, he heard his voice echo back. It seemed to be echoing inside the wall.

"Here I am Pedro", he shouted again. And this time he was sure the echo was from inside the wall.

At that moment Pedro appeared.

"Oh, here you are, Sir", he smiled, "I have some news for you. Caetano says that the young *Conde* was a very cruel man. His name was Henri".

Lino kept silent, pondering over what Pedro had revealed.

"Did he know Henri before he came to Goa?" asked Lino after some time.

"No sir, interestingly, the Conde had never brought his family to Goa earlier", said Pedro.

At that moment Lino suddenly remembered what he was investigating. He showed Pedro the dried drops of blood. Lino tapped the wall with a decorative dagger which was hanging on the wall and told Pedro to listen to the echo. Soon Pedro and Lino were on the lookout for the concealed opening into the secret room. After turning over the two paintings on the wall, they noticed a peg which appeared to be for hanging pictures. After pulling down on the peg a clicking sound was heard as if a latch had disengaged. Lino pushed at the section of wall and as expected, it opened inwards. Inside they saw a long dark tunnel.

He asked Pedro to get a candle. After Pedro had returned with a lit candle, the Captain took it from him and insisted on leading the way. Suddenly, some dark shapes seemed to rush at them. In a quick reflex action, both Lino as well as Pedro ducked down. They were just some harmless bats disturbed from their slumber.

As they went around a bend, a few paces in front of them, they saw a strip of light on the ground. It was obviously a door. Lino pushed the door inwards and as he entered, he saw the light filtering from a window in the wall.

Lino was shocked to see a bloodstained stone in the centre of the room with a human skull on it. An eerie looking statue stood in a corner next to a window. There was also a small fireplace where a brass pot was hanging.

"Oh my Lord, what a scary place!" exclaimed Pedro. Lino was quiet as he scanned the room.

He had a shocked expression on his face. After pacing the room, he stopped at a niche, where he found some rag dolls.

"I wonder who used to practice voodoo in this household", he said.

"It has been used recently too", said Pedro.

Lino, on a sudden impulse went back to the niche and pocketed the dolls.

"Pedro, where are you?" he called.

"Master, don't touch anything. I feel a lot of evil has taken place here. Let's leave", he said uncomfortably.

...❧♦❧...

Back at the Abranches mansion, Lino was sitting in the balcony outside his room. In his hand he had two rag dolls; one was of a man and the other of a woman. He remembered putting them in his pocket. But as he was about to see them closely, Pedro came in.

"Hello Pedro, good to see you. I am anxious to know the news. Did you find out whether the *Conde* was ever in Africa?" Lino asked him excitedly, trying to find out who it was that was practicing voodoo.

"Yes sir, according to Caetano, he came directly from Portugal. He knows that because he had once heard him asking one of the African slaves about the place. He said that he always wanted to go there", Pedro told him.

"That is very interesting?" commented Lino.

"And his son Henri came from Macau", said Pedro.

"Anything more?" asked Lino, dejected that neither of them had connections with Africa.

"Yes sir, Caetano told me that the Conde de Almeida and two other servants, including the lone African slave died of mysterious circumstances during the time Henri landed in Goa", Pedro told him.

"You did a good job, Pedro", commented Lino.

"The old man used to be good to Caetano, who attended to him because the Conde couldn't see too well. In fact, the Conde had asked his son to come to Goa because of this fact. He wanted him to settle some pending matters for him. It was said that the Conde de Almeida did keep on repeating "Henri has indeed changed, Caetano. He was always such a gentle child".

When Pedro left, he started playing with the dolls unconsciously while his mind was on the hideout. "I wonder who practiced voodoo and who the two dolls represent", he said to himself the moment he became aware of the dolls in his hand.

He had heard from one of his African soldiers many years ago, how the voodoo witchdoctors stuck pins and committed other atrocities through dolls of the victims. They believed that this would cause the same pain in the victims. Usually the dolls contained a piece of clothing or hair of the victim they were to torture. Now as the captain looked at the doll of the man, he had a gut feeling that it was of him. The lock of hair seemed to match his closely but he wasn't sure.

"The other must have been that of Paula", he said to himself, "I remember that she had a dress of this colour".

But he couldn't understand how the Conde or his son Henri be connected to either of them. " . . . Unless Henri was somehow involved with Herodiana!" Lino exclaimed aloud.

Lino wasted no time in pursuing this new possibility. He knew that the only person who would notice any strange happenings in the house would be Preta, as she was always around. So he called for Preta for he was sure that she must have seen Herodiana's lover closely.

"Preta, can you please tell me about the man who used to come to see the Lady?" he asked her.

At first, she was totally taken aback by the direct question. She looked scared and embarrassed at the same time. Then, realizing it was safe to speak out the truth, told him everything about Herodiana's affair with Bufon. "The Lady always referred to him as Amorous", she told him.

"Did you ever see his horse", asked the Captain.

"Yes sir . . . at stable. He bad man . . . he touch me", she told him softly.

"Well, can you describe his horse?" he asked eagerly.

"The horse different . . . black, white tail and white patch around eyes", she told him hesitatingly, as she struggled to describe the image in her mind.

That evening, Lino went to the horse market. He knew a couple of Arab dealers there.

"*Capitao*, what brings you here?" one of them hailed him as he walked past a stall.

"Oh! Hello Hussein. I am looking for a horse with a white tail and white patches around its eyes. Do you remember selling such a horse to anybody?" he asked.

But the Arab dealer could not recollect any horse as described. As he was pondering over what to do next, he saw a large crowd gathered around a merchant whose stall was in a corner at the end of the row.

Out of curiosity, he went to see what was happening. The crowd made way for him, because he had worn his army uniform. When he reached in front, he couldn't believe his eyes. "*Mae De Deus*!" He exclaimed, as he saw the very same horse which Preta had described. It was indeed a majestic horse.

"Can you please tell me who sold you this horse?" Lino asked him in a stern voice. The dealer felt intimidated by the iron ring in his voice, and was eager to give the information he sought. The description the horse dealer gave him fitted that of Amorous.

"I believe the owner left with his family for Portugal two weeks ago. The person who sold it to me worked for him. Its owner was a Conde", said the dealer.

Now Lino was sure that the Conde and Amorous Bufon, the man who was his wife's lover, were the one and same man. At last he had a good lead to his daughter.

"I wonder if he knows that she is Paula's daughter", he thought to himself, as he decided to go to Portugal and get the child back.

...❧◆❧...

After an arduous journey, which would have ended up in a fight with a large Dutch armada, Lino finally arrived in Lisboa.

Stepping onto home soil, he felt a sudden sadness engulf him. He realised now how much Goa had meant to him. He felt that he was in a foreign land . . . He indeed missed the golden land of swaying palms, sun-drenched beaches and verdant hills.

He had a few friends there but he didn't want to contact them till it was completely necessary. Instead, he went straight to the army headquarters to collect his pass to the company quarters. He had planned his trip meticulously to the finest detail. First he had to get in touch with Bufon and find out if he would cooperate and handover

Paulina to him without trouble. If he resisted, he would then have to file a case in the court to get her back. Although Lino did not know how it would all pan out, he had faith that Paula was surely there with him to guide him through all this.

"Lino! Good to see you. Welcome home, son! We are proud to have valiant men like you, who through their sacrifice shine for our country" said the elderly officer who was in charge of the infantry guarding the city". What brings you here son?"

"I am on Personal business, Sir. I may need a good lawyer for that later. But right now, I would be obliged if I could stay at the officers' mess", the Captain replied.

"Of course, Captain", he said, and rang the bell for his subordinates. A young lieutenant with a smiling face entered the room. The Colonel introduced the Captain and asked him to provide him with the best room available and anything else that was needed to make his stay comfortable.

The Lieutenant saluted smartly and led Lino to a beautiful suite with views over the River Tagus, "Sir, This is the best we can offer you sir. We hope you like the room. I will have your luggage brought in and then see that the place is cleaned up", he told the Captain.

After a bath and a good night's sleep, he got himself a good horse and rode to the place where Paula's mother lived. He asked for directions to *Castello Santo Jorge* and rode in that direction. To his surprise, it was not far from the port at the foot-hill, exactly as Paula had described stood the quaint old cottage.

As he approached it, he was nervous. "What will I tell her mother?" he wondered. But as he drew close, he saw that the place looked deserted and the garden was overgrown. As he tried to open the rusty gate, in a corner, he saw an old ship's wheel. He picked it up and saw the names—Rosalia, Henri and Paula carved on it.

As he walked up to the verandah, he pictured Paula as a little girl. "I am sure she was a pretty girl back then. She must have been sitting here as she did on the hill in Goa, watching the sea", he muttered to himself

He sat on the porch and hid his face in his hands". Oh, Paula! Where will I find another you?" he said aloud.

"Yes sir, Paula is irreplaceable. But who, may I ask, are you?" said a young female voice from behind him.

Lino was startled to hear the sweet voice and almost uttered Paula's name. Lost in his own thoughts, he had not been aware of the presence of another person.

Lino looked up to see a pretty girl who appeared to be in her teens standing in front of him.

"I am Helena, who are you?" she asked boldly.

The name rang a bell in his mind. And suddenly he remembered that Paula had told him about the young girl who lived in her neighbourhood.

"Helena, I have heard about you. Paula spoke about you", he told her, "I am Lino and Paula stayed at my house in Goa".

"Lino!" she exclaimed, moving back in disbelief. Tears were flowing from her eyes.

"Who would have thought Paula would never come back. I still remember that last night I coaxed her to dance that Goan dance. It was both a happy as well as sad occasion. Happy because that was the last time our families were all together and sad because Paula was leaving", she told him, dabbing the tears with a handkerchief.

Lino who was in tears too, asked her about Paula's mother.

"Sir, she died just two months ago. It was soon after she received the terrible letter of Paula's death". Helena informed him. She explained further, "She went into a depression and refused to eat anything".

...ᷞ◆ᷞ...

After meeting Helena's parents, the heavy-hearted Lino went back to his room and early next morning, he was out again, breathing in the pure air of the countryside. The architecture of the place reminded him so much of Goa.

After about an hour, he came to the *Castello De Almeida*. He dismounted at the gate and through the peephole introduced himself to the guards. The mighty gate was opened and he was led inside by two armed guards who saluted him.

The residing Conde was an elderly man. "He must be Conde Henri's brother", Lino said to himself.

"I am Salazar", the aristocratic man said with a smile, "What brings you here, Captain?"

"Sir, I came to meet your nephew Henri. I think, he and his family have just arrived from Portugal", Lino told him. The old man seemed surprised.

"Henri is here . . . my God! Why didn't anyone tell me? In fact I had sent word to him soon after the death of his father to come and settle the inheritance issues" he said aloud and then called out for his valet.

"Lucio, do you know anything about the arrival of my nephew Henri?" he asked the valet who had come on the double.

"No sir, not yet", he replied.

"Thank you, Lucio, and one other thing. We have a guest for lunch today", the Conde told him with a look in Lino's direction. Though Lino told him that he was leaving, the Conde insisted that he dine with him, saying, "It is not very often that I have a guest".

So Lino obliged, and they then spoke about the cold war with the Dutch Navy and how the Portuguese were expanding their kingdom in the east.

The Conde also wanted to know about Goa for he always wanted to go there, but he had somehow never fulfilled that desire. He had served mostly in Brazil.

"I wonder where Henri lives now" Lino said to himself as he rode back to his barracks, after a sumptuous lunch at the Conde's castle. "Did he really come to Portugal? Is he really the Conde d'Almeida? If he is, then why didn't he lay claim to the title?" These questions arose in his mind.

Meanwhile, Henri alias Amorous Bufon was indeed in Portugal. His wife Amarella and their little daughter Paulina were with him too. They had arrived a little less than a month before Lino. However, Bufon had lied to his wife Amarella that he couldn't visit the Almeida Castle, because his father had some problem with his younger brother, the present Conde.

But the real reason why Bufon was avoiding the visit was, because he had found out that the present Conde was Henri's youngest uncle. So he was scared that the old man would recognise him. When he had befriended Henri he had learnt that Henri had spent most of his time in Goa and then in Macau. However, at that time, Bufon didn't have the patience to get all the information and now wasn't sure whether Henri had ever visited Portugal. At the first opportunity he had murdered the poor man and assumed his identity.

Now he regretted doing that. Not the killing, but for not getting enough information out of Henri! Suddenly a thought came to his mind. "The only way to make sure that the Conde did not recognise him was to get rid of him. But first I have to send Amarella and the girl to her relatives".

So a month after their arrival, Amarella had a chance to go to visit her relatives. For a long time, Bufon wanted to avoid going there because he didn't like to live with any family.

They were accorded a warm welcome and little Paulina made a great impression on the Cabrals. After about a week, Bufon told Amarella that he had to see some lawyers in Lisboa. And saying this he rode out of the palatial residence of his wife's cousins.

"I know how to find Henri", Lino said to himself suddenly, as he prepared to go to bed. "I am sure he must have gone to his wife's relatives place".

He referred to his notes and he found out that Amarella was the daughter of Leonar de Cabral, a colonel in the army.

The next day, the army records led him to Leonar de Cabral's residence, in Belem, which was not far from Lisbon. Without wasting time he rode to the Cabral residence.

"Oh! The gentleman is not in right now, but his Lady is. Please sit here sir, what can I say is the purpose of your visit? And your name, sir?" asked the butler politely.

"I am Captain Abranches of the Portuguese army and I have just arrived from Goa. Tell her I know Henri from his army days", he bluffed.

After some time, the Captain came face to face with a beautiful lady, who had entered the room.

"Hello Sir, I am Amarella, Henri's wife", she said offering her hand.

The Captain took it in his and kissed it gently. "I want to meet him urgently", he told her. "Do you know where he can be found?" He asked graciously.

She was very obliging and told him to check the Nacional Hotel in Lisboa where they had been staying ever since they came to Portugal.

Suddenly a small child entered shouting excitedly, "Mama, mama, come to see what I made".

Lino's heart sank and he felt his knees trembling, when he saw the child. She was the exact copy of his beloved Paula.

Her eyes were turquoise blue and her flowing blonde hair was tied in plaits, which fenced with each other as she ran back to where she came from, after staring at him. Lino was so overwhelmed with emotion that he quickly excused himself and left the room in great haste without waiting for the lady to courtesy.

"What a rude man!" Lady Amarella muttered to herself. Luckily she had not seen his reaction when he looked at Paulina.

The Captain rode for a few kilometers and then sat down on a rock nearby. He was feeling weak, as thoughts of Paula flooded his heart. "Oh Paula, what a beautiful child you left behind. Oh God! I must have my child back!" he cried.

After Bufon had left the Cabral House, he had gone straight to his hotel room. There he set up his voodoo altar. It was a full moon night, so it was ideal for him to start his dark rites. After chanting some versus in Swahili he stuck needles into a doll. It was fashioned out of strips from the Conde's old clothes which he had received from a bribed day servant at the mansion. He continued this for the next few nights. But after a week, he got frustrated that there was no news of the Conde's death or sickness. Somehow the man had withstood his most powerful spell.

As he was nursing his anger, he heard a knock on the door. Hurriedly he closed the bathroom door, where he was performing the rites. He was not expecting anyone and so he deliberately took his own time to open the door. A tall handsome man stood at the door.

Alarm bells went off in his evil head for he recognised the Captain almost immediately. He had seen him the night Herodiana had drugged him in order to satisfy her fantasy of making love whilst her husband was sleeping on the same bed.

For a moment he froze and then grimaced as if in pain.

Lino had never seen Bufon, so he was a little taken aback by the giant of a man. But he composed himself. The face of little Paulina made his anger surface again. He took in a deep breath and calmed himself.

Bufon was watching him intently; he had absolutely no intention to start a conversation.

"I am Captain Lino Abranches. May I come in?" he asked, trying a most courteous voice.

But Bufon had no respect for people. He just made a snorting sound and remained blocking the entry into the house.

The Captain was beginning to see red. Now he forgot all his manners and shouted at him, "Henri, I believe that you adopted a baby from the *Recolhimento da Nossa Sr. de Terra*".

"Yes, I have. Is that any concern of yours?" growled Bufon.

"That child is mine", said the Captain, suddenly softening the tone of his voice and trying to be humble because he wanted the child desperately. He realised that if this man could see reason, he could avoid dragging it out in court.

"Your child", said Bufon, laughing louder than before, "Prove that it is your child. Paulina is now our child. We have legally adopted her in Goa".

"But you can't do that . . ." started Lino, but even as he said it, he knew that this was going to be a tough legal battle.

"Don't speak to me. Speak to my lawyer", Bufon cut him short and slammed the door.

Bufon didn't think much about Lino's visit. He felt that the case would just be laughed at. So he focused more on his bid for the title of the Almeida Castle. Since his voodoo magic was not working on the Conde, he braced himself for the first visit to the castle.

Meanwhile Lino had already sent the legal notices to Bufon. And the case was to be heard at the Court. He hadn't much documentation with him, but he had sent a message to Pedro and some trusted friends in Goa.

That evening Lino received a message from the Conde asking him to meet him urgently. When he went there, he found the Conde in a very disturbed mood. Bufon had paid him a visit. The old man had been happy to see his nephew for the first time but he was heartbroken when Henri didn't even greet him politely. He told him straightaway that he had come to take back what belonged to his father.

As he narrated all this to the captain, the latter suddenly remembered the conversation with Caetano at Bufon's residence in Goa. According to him, the old Conde had found him so different from the Henri he knew as a child. But all who questioned his identity had died mysterious deaths. The voodoo room in Bufon's residence also came to his mind, but he kept silent.

"Does he look like the Henri you knew?" Lino suddenly asked the Conde after their meal.

"No, during that time I was shipwrecked on an island and then after many months, when at last I was picked up by a passing ship I came to Goa. It is a long story, but one that I will tell you someday if you permit me", replied the Conde.

"Then who do you think can identify him?" the Captain asked.

After thinking for a few minutes, the Conde told him that their old *scrivao* Germano who was looking after the house in his absence would know him.

"He lives nearby. I will send the carriage to collect him. I will see you later, Captain", said the Conde.

Chapter 15

NEW BEGINNINGS

A mong the people present in the large courtroom, Lino knew only Helena and her parents and the Conde de Almeida. But that didn't disturb him at all. What made his heart race was the child he was trying to gain custody of—innocent little Paulina. "What was her fault? What had she done to deserve all this?" he asked himself. But then, he realised that he had to take her away. Deep down, he felt there was another reason for adopting Paulina but he could just not figure it out.

His thoughts were disturbed by the entrance of the judge. He rapped his gavel for order and called for the plaintiff and defendant.

"Suit is filed for custody of the child, Paulina. Plaintiff requests the court for immediate modification of the child's birth registration", stated Lino.

"What is your defence to claim the child?" asked the judge turning to Lino.

"It is all in the plaint, your honour", said Lino who had decided at the very last minute to defend himself with the help of legal councel.

"How can you prove that the child is yours? Sufficient document and evidence is required. If not, the case has to be withdrawn with cost to be levied on the plaintiff", warned the judge.

"Honouring your request, I will satisfy your Lordship that this child is mine", said Lino confidently.

"Under the law, once the child is given in adoption, there is no clause to reinstate the child to the so called parent unless the evidence is strong enough to sustain the case", the judge clarified.

"With due respect, my lord, and sufficient evidence to augment my statements I will proceed with the case", Lino confirmed.

"But it was three years after the birth of the child and after the murder of Paula, that I found her diary". The judge looked at the worn leather diary that was handed to him. After reading the diary, the judge declared, "Well, this appears to support what you said. But then it does not connect to this particular child in any way. But tell me, is this child born out of this illicit relationship?"

Lino hesitated and said slowly," yes my lord".

"You may sit now", ordered the judge. Then turning to Amorous Bufon, who was now in the dock, the judge addressed him, "How did you find the child?"

"My wife and I decided to adopt a child since we were told that she could never bear children. Therefore we went to the closest orphanage and enquired if there was a Portuguese girl available for adoption and Paulina was introduced to us. We at once knew that she was the right one for us", said Bufon confidently.

"Why did you like this particular child?" The judge asked.

"We thought it would be impossible to get a Portuguese child for adoption. When we learnt of Paula, there was no doubt that the child was God sent to us!"

"At the time of processing the registration of the child, what was your opinion of the child?"

"Paulina was absolutely gorgeous and there was no doubt that she was formed of decent European parents".

"Did you have any clue as to who the parents were and what must have been the history of the child?" Asked the judge.

"We knew the story only beginning from the hospital".

What were the parent's names on the record?

"Just Paula and maybe my grandmother"

Were the whereabouts of the parents known to you at the time of adoption?"

"No clue was given. We were told that the mother's name was Melissa and she passed away in an accident. The name of the father was nowhere on record. In fact we were told that this child was born out of an illicit relationship.

"On record what was the designation of the mother? What was her means of livelihood at the time of delivery?"

"The case history told us that the mother was living in Goa, a single woman of ill repute who had no set job and could barely support the child. We were told that the child was abandoned in Goa on the beach after the mother's death and the villagers were looking after her. The priest of the village took this child and kept her in the orphanage and there, the priest had registered the name of this child and her mother's".

How old is the child now? Is she here in the courtroom?"

After a signal from Bufon, Lady Amarella came forward with little Paulina. "Here is our daughter, your honour. She is three years old", said Bufon, pointing out to her.

The judge signalled to them to go back to their seats.

"After the Superior of the orphanage agreed to give us this child in adoption we completed the documentation.

We registered her under the Act of Adoption in the Registration of Rights under the Law of Goa, as her foster parents and kept a surety to say that we would not use the child for any trade or any unscrupulous activity. We found that Goa was not a proper place for the child, so we decided to bring her to Portugal".

"Does the child know you as her foster parents? Does she go to school?"

"No, she is too young to understand. She knows nothing about us being her foster parents. We have just arrived here and intend finding a tutor for her soon".

"What is your attitude towards the child?"

"We treat her as our own child and we love her and she loves us".

"I take it that you and your wife understand that if the plaintiff proves that the child is his, you will have to part with this child?"

"At no cost will we part with this child. She is ours now", Bufon retorted. He paused nervously and then continued, "Depends on the reaction of the child. As for us, we are reluctant to release this child, even if sufficient evidence is produced".

"The Plaintiff, please approach the bench", declared the judge, turning to Lino, as Amorous took his seat.

"What is your stand? Defend your case if you really want the child. Where were you all these years?"

"Your honour, I was unaware or rather ignorant that I had a child through Paula", Lino told the judge. "Paula was murdered by my wife, who then committed suicide. I became an unfaithful husband, only after I came to know that she had a lover. But then, my heart was broken after I discovered that my wife had numerous abortions. That is when I gave in to my feelings for Paula. She had left the house when she discovered she was pregnant. I didn't know anything about it. And it was by God's grace that I found her in the Convent of Santa Monica", he told the judge, telling about Sr. Magdalena and how she had helped her to keep the child at the Recolhimento.

"Then why didn't you bring the child home?"

"Well, I didn't know about it. According to Sr. Magdalena, the Assistant Prioress of the Convent, Paulina was kept in the orphanage because Paula had plans to bring her to Portugal".

"Does anyone here know Paula? Are any of her parents living?"

Lino looked at the crowd and was happy to see Helena raise her hands in the audience.

The judge invited her to come forward and she did so.

"Yes, your honour, my family knows Paula. None of her parents are living. The mother died of depression recently after she heard about the death of her only daughter", said Helena.

"But do you know Captain Lino here?"

"Paula wrote to me, about Captain Lino and how wonderful he was", she declared.

"Your honour, in her last letter Paula wrote to us about Captain Lino and said that he deserved to have a better life. At first I didn't understand what she meant by it. But now I know after hearing the whole story", Helena continued.

"Thank you. You may please be seated", said the judge. Then turning to Lino, he continued, "How long were you married? Tell us about yourself"

"I have been married for over a decade. I am a Captain in the King's army in Goa. Besides the army salary, my family owns a lot of property."

"How many children do you have?"

"As I mentioned earlier, my wife didn't want children at all. In fact, according to the Church, my marriage would be considered null and void, your honour".

"What is your *locus standi* at present? What is your plea?"

"I stand before you, your honour, believing that I will be able to prove my case. I know that I can get sufficient evidence to claim my child! I request six months to travel to Goa and back"

"I grant you six months during which time; the child will remain in custody of the foster parents. The foster parents will not be allowed to change residence during this time without first informing the court. The next hearing will be after six months. You will be informed of the date and time for our next session. The Court is adjourned".

Many thoughts ran through Lino's mind on the return journey to Goa. He backtracked into all the happenings in Goa and one single person stood out as being a key to solving the whole puzzle. Adeline the midwife had been missing from Morjim for quite some time and no one knew her whereabouts. Lino decided that he had to find her at any cost and take her statement regarding her conversations with Paula.

As soon as Lino arrived in Goa, he told Pedro to make arrangements for a boat to take them to Morjim the very next morning.

The next day was going to be a Sunday. Isidore and Bella suddenly came up with a bright idea to meet the chaplain and request him to announce a message to the people at the end of every mass. Almost all of the people in Morjim were converts to Christianity and dutifully attended Sunday mass without fail. There had to be someone who would know something of Adeline's whereabouts.

The chaplain was a kind old priest who travelled to Morjim every week to offer mass on Sundays. After Lino explained in brief about his plight, He was very accommodating and at once agreed to make the necessary announcements.

The announcements were made at all services that Sunday. But nobody came forward with any information on Adeline. The chaplain was kind enough to repeat the announcement the next Sunday. Early next morning, as Bella was preparing to go to the beach to pick up fish for the days sale, there was a knock on the door. Santan, a well known farmer from their village, stood smiling at the door.

"Santan! What brings you here this early in the morning? Please do come in", said Bella, and called out to Isidore, who was inside the kitchen, lighting up the twigs for their morning *chai*.

"I came regarding the church announcement made this week. I was at the City when it was made and I only heard it yesterday from Lorna", said Santan.

Isidore who had joined the two was anxious to know what Santan had to say and asked him to go on.

"I remember very clearly that morning, three years back when Adeline came to my house with her sister Rosa and a baby asking me to take them to the City hospital urgently because the baby was not keeping well. On the way, I had to oblige although I was really busy with the harvesting arrangements. That day, whilst I was taking them to the city, I overheard them talking in low tones and I could only hear Adeline telling her sister to go to her aunt's place on the island of Divar, just across the Cidade, on the opposite banks of the River Mandovi. I tried to make conversation with them, but they only responded in monosyllables".

"Is there anything else you can say about them? It is really important that we know", said Pedro hopefully.

"The best thing to do is to look for Adeline's sister in Divar. Being a small place, someone or the other will be able to locate them", said Santan. Although Bella offered to serve coffee, Santan graciously refused and left saying he had many tasks to complete before the close of day.

The news regarding Adeline and Rosa was music to Lino's ears. Pedro, Lino and Isidore who had come with the news, decided to leave for Divar immediately. There wasn't much information that would lead them to Adeline but at least they could try.

The boatman at the Cidade dock was a young and talkative boy who was used to ferrying many picnicking Portuguese families to the island. Being a local himself, he immediately struck a conversation with Pedro and Isidore, as he rowed across the Mandovi. One thing good that came out of the mundane conversation was that his father knew every person on the island and could even remember the family lineage of the villagers. When this was conveyed to Lino, his eyes at once brightened up and wanted to meet with his father immediately. After tipping the boy handsomely, they alighted from the canoe and followed the boatman to a little hut beside the ferry point, where an old man sat mending his '*coblem*', a trap used to catch crabs.

After the boy had introduced them to him, he asked without even lifting his eyes off from his needle, "What can I do for you sirs?"

"We are looking for a certain Rosa Fernandes who may be living with her aunt here. All I can say is that she may have come to live with her aunt some three years ago with a baby", said Pedro.

"There are at least four women that I can remember who share that name. Is there anything else you can tell me that will help me guide you better?" He asked, taking a long drag at his home rolled tobacco cigar. Pedro looked at Isidore and Lino quizzically. Then Isisdore suddenly remembered that they had not mentioned Adeline's name.

"*Pai*, we also know that Rosa has a sister named Adeline. She is a midwife by profession", said Isidore.

"Oh that poor lady! I remember now! She was married to that drunk, Rogtao who troubled her to death. She fled from him one day and was not to be heard of. Yes, now I know which family you are talking about. Their aunt lives in the house close to the Divar church. Go and ask for Divina. She is a wellknown midwife of this village", said the old man, pointing to the huge church at the top of the hill, peeping out through the trees.

The house was easy to locate. Divina was a heavily built elderly lady of about 65 years. She was in the '*balcao*' of her house, darning a tear on a blouse. Isidore immediately recognized Rosa, who was cleaning some rice. Rosa did not appear to be very pleased seeing Isidore for some reason however, it was too late to hide from them as she was already noticed. This time Isidore did the round of introductions and the three of them settled down on the stone seats in the balcao.

"Rosa, you are exactly the person we wanted to meet. Morjim has been without our dear midwife Adeline and no one knows what has happened to her. Maybe you can help us find her?" said Isidore, getting straight to the point.

Rosa shifted uncomfortably in her chair. All she said was", I wish I knew where my sister disappeared. I hope she has not killed herself. No one knows where she is. It has been three long years since she went missing".

Lino then reminded Isidore that Rosa was present at the delivery of Paulina. He asked him to question her regarding that.

At the mention of Paula, Rosa's face turned white with fear but she quickly composed herself and said, "Yes, I was living with her for a short while in Morjim. She was living a very lonely life and needed company. Paula came in for her delivery and I helped arrange all the towels and utensils for the birth but I was not allowed to enter the room until Paula had delivered the . . ." Rosa paused in midsentence.

Suddenly, as if led by a deep inner voice, Lino convinced Pedro to tell the whole story of his love affair with Paula. Although Pedro found it unnecessary, at his master's insistence, he told Rosa the whole story, without leaving out any details. For some strange reason Rosa burst out crying when she was told that Lino's chances of getting Paulina back were slim if he did not find convincing evidence to prove that Paulina was really his daughter.

"Is there anything you remember about Adeline that we can carry out a search for her ourselves? I am a Captain in the army and I can arrange a top level search for Adeline. All I ask is for information to narrow down the search. I have very little time to find the evidence", said Lino pleadingly.

"Adeline is believed dead. The police have already done their best three years back. They even found a decomposed body that went unidentified to this day and I believe it was her", said Rosa very firmly.

Lino was disappointed and turned around to leave. Pedro and Isidore thanked Rosa and Divina on his behalf and followed suit. There was not much that they could do now and Paulina was as good as lost.

Lino decided to make the trip back to Portugal although he could see the outcome. It was a lost case. It could well be the last time he would see Paulina. Although the sea was calm, he was facing a raging storm within himself.

One day, as Lino was lounging on the upper deck of the galleon, suddenly he heard Paula speak to him as if in a dream", My love, I have tried to explain the power of faith to you many times however you have never given me the chance. Remember Hebrews 11:1?"

Lino got up with a start. Why was Paula bringing to mind the scripture now? Reluctantly, he went to talk to a Jesuit missionary who was returning to Portugal from Goa.

After introducing himself to the priest, he asked if he could shed some light on this particular scripture that was now coming to him again and again.

"My son, what do you see in my hand?" He asked Lino.

"A pen father", replied Lino, trying to contain his impatience.

"Now what am I holding son?" Asked Fr. Savio, removing the pen from his fingers but still keeping the grip as if holding an imaginary pen.

"Nothing Father, but what is the point you are making Father?" Asked Lino, showing a little irritation.

"With my eyes of faith, I can see a pen son!" He replied victoriously. "The Bible in the letter to the Hebrews, defines faith as being 'the assurance of things hoped for, and the conviction of things not yet seen.' Going by your senses, you believe I have a pen in my hand because you can see with your eyes and feel with your hands that it is a pen. Therefore you believe. Biblical faith is not that!

First you believe that what you have prayed for has been received and then you will have what you confess with your mouth".

"But Padre, how do I apply the teaching in my situation Father?" Asked Lino, getting a little attracted to the concept of Faith. Lino updated Fr. Savio about the court case and how he is sure to lose Paulina".

"Death and life are in the power of the tongue; and they that love it shall eat the fruit thereof", said Fr. Savio, quoting from book of Proverbs of the Bible. "Always prophecy how you want to see the end result and keep that image in your mind. Keep on confessing the result in the name of Jesus, and you will have what you say".

"But Father, how do I know it works?" asked Lino skeptically.

"My son, you have nothing to lose right? Just try it for what it is worth, and then you will see the glory of God!" said Fr. Savio, with conviction.

...❦◆❦...

A smiling and relaxed Lino sat in the courtroom, waiting for the judge to enter and begin the day's proceedings. Helena and her father were there too. But they were very tense at the thought of Lino losing the whole battle. But strangely, Lino seemed to be totally guaranteed of winning the case. He seemed to be totally at rest and even winked at them, assuring them with a smile that all was going to be well.

As the judge entered, Lino had one last look at the two scriptures which he had written on top of his file. By faith he had renewed his mind and had already formed the picture of returning to Goa with Paulina. With his tongue he confessed that Paulina was his forever in the name of Jesus.

"Plaintiff, will you please step forward?" called the judge.

Lino approached the bench. "I hope you have sufficient evidence to balance your statement and prove your right over the child, if you are zealous to have the custody of the child", said the judge.

"My lord, I wish to tell you that it is my ardent desire to prove to you that the child is mine. As mentioned earlier, I had a difficult marriage. When I met Paula, who had joined our family as a lady-in-waiting it was our common interest in poetry and painting, which attracted us. She came from a respectable Catholic family and felt it was wrong to have an affair with a married man. Then I discovered how my wife had been aborting my babies. I also came to know she had a lover". Lino told the judge softly, as he paused to look at Bufon, who avoided his stare.

"Go on", urged the judge.

"I told Paula about it as she was my only friend. One day, she was kidnapped and I rescued her after finding out where she was housed. That's when we manifested our love physically for the first time. At that moment, we didn't feel guilty about it, because the feelings for each other were overwhelming and uncontrollable. After that, she disappeared again; I think it was because she found out she was pregnant. She didn't want my wife to have a reason to embarrass me. I agree that I delayed the divorce, but then I was called on by headquarters to go on a secret mission. That's the time my wife lured Paula to the cliff by substituting my note with one of her own. Paula was then pushed off the cliff . . ." he continued and stopped, choked with emotion.

The judge looked at him for a moment and then asked, "Do you know of anybody who knew about your relationship with her?"

"Yes, my valet, Pedro knew about it. In fact he knows the entire story, as he was a witness to everything", said Lino.

Just when the judge was about to tell him to continue, Bufon stood up and interjected, "Objection, your honour! Where is his witness?"

The judge turned to Lino, "Sir, can you provide proof of this. Do you have any written statement?"

The Captain's face fell and he looked down. Bufon looked victorious.

"Your honour, do you need a written statement? Won't it suffice to have the witness present in flesh and blood?" said a new voice, appearing from the midst of the crowded courtroom.

Bufon's jaw fell when he saw Pedro standing there. And the Captain couldn't believe his eyes.

"Who are you?" asked the judge, noting that Pedro was a non-European.

"I am Pedro and I have been working for the Captain for a very long time. Before that, my mother worked for the family", said Pedro.

"Well, Pedro, can you tell us what you know about Captain Lino?"

"Captain Lino is a gentleman and an officer with a great record. The entire staff of the Abranches household will stand by that. In fact, here is a statement with their thumb prints on it", said the faithful friend of the Abranches family, handing over a parchment to the judge.

So, Pedro gave a statement which exactly matched the Captain's.

"This has all been made up", shouted Bufon.

"Silence in my Court! Please don't talk out of turn!" ordered the judge firmly. Then, turning to Pedro he enquired, "Where were you during the last court session?"

"I was in Goa, Sir. In fact, I just arrived a few hours ago. Here are my identification papers and proof of my journey", said Pedro.

"All is fine and matches with what this gentleman has just said", declared the judge, looking at Bufon who remained silent.

"Have you seen Paula's child and can you identify her?" he asked Pedro.

"Honestly I cannot Sir, because we didn't know about the child, until the Master found the diary. After that . . ."

"That will be enough, you can sit down now", said the judge, with a faint smile. He was pleased with Pedro's honesty.

The judge then told Bufon to approach the bench and said to him, "According to the plaintiff, you have no house in Portugal. Is that true?"

"I am the Conde de Almeida and I have an appealed to the court, to legalize my father's title".

"Objection, your honour", said an elderly gentleman from the audience.

The judge looked up and at once recognised the Conde de Almeida. "Please approach the bench", he said.

"I agree Sir, that my elder brother's son has a right to the title. But the problem is, that this man is not that son", declared the Conde in a clear voice.

There was an immediate hush inside the courtroom as everyone waited with abated breath as to where this new development would lead this case.

"Why do you say that sir?" asked the judge.

"Your honour, may I call on the caretaker of our property, Senhor Germano?"

"Senhor Germano, please approach the bench", stated the judge.

Bufon's heart was racing now. 'Could this gentleman have known the real Henri?' he wondered, as the old man walked up slowly.

"Your honour, all I can say is that this man is not my Henri. I don't know who he is. But he is not Henri", he said in a trembling voice.

"Objection! Your honour! What case is being discussed here? How does my status affect this child? Look at her. Does she look starved? Haven't I paid for her journey here? We travelled first class mind you. I can pay for her upkeep. And how can you take one man's word that I am not the Conde?"

The judge quieted the murmurs in the courtroom, while he consulted the jury. Then, after awhile, he addressed the audience.

"I don't know whether the gentleman is Henri or not. For that is another case. Right now, I didn't find any substantial evidence that Paulina is Captain Lino's child. Bufon has the necessary documentation that he legally adopted the child. So in the Name of the King, the Court declares . . ."

"Wait, your honour, I can prove that Paulina is the Captain's daughter!" shouted a woman who had just entered the courtroom. Next to her was a child whose head was covered with a veil.

Everyone was stunned. The Captain was totally confused. Pedro joined his hands and prayed that this woman would have something worthwhile to say that would reverse the judgment in their favour.

Bufon glared at the woman but he couldn't recollect who she would be. "Approach the bench quickly and tell me who you are", stated the Judge, sounding impatient. He was a person who wouldn't leave any stone unturned while meting out justice. "Sir, I am the midwife who delivered the baby Paulina", she said.

"Can she prove that?" asked Bufon.

"Yes, she had a mole under her right armpit" said the woman.

"Please verify it".

The judge looked at the document. Then he told one of the lady jurors to take Paulina and check the identifying mark.

There was silence now and Bufon and Lady Amarella grew restless. The lady jury re-entered the Court room and declared, "This little girl has a mole under her right armpit as mentioned by this lady".

The audience started clapping. They were really intrigued by the whole case. In fact, they had been sad that the decision was going against the Captain. They had observed the genuine sadness on the Captain's face. The way Bufon was conducting himself; it looked like his happiness was not in getting the child back, but in striking back at the Captain. Now they were filled with hope that things would turn in the Captain's favour.

"Also", continued Adeline "here is the actual proof of my statement". As she said these words, she removed the veil from the little girl who was standing next to her. The whole courtroom gasped at the amazing likeness to Paulina.

"This is Lavina", she added.

Lino could not believe his eyes. Pedro almost fell off his chair.

Everyone was awestruck. Lavina was an exact copy of Paulina. And this comparison was obvious to all when the lady juror brought Paulina forward and made her stand next to Lavina.

"One last question", declared the judge who looked relieved now. For even he was sure that the Captain was telling the truth, but he just didn't have the evidence. "How is it that you have this child?"

Adeline hung her head in shame and whispered, "Forgive me, Paula". Then she looked up and said, "Sir, I didn't have children of my own. I always wanted a daughter. And when I assisted Paula's delivery and discovered that she had twins, an idea hit me. I took the help of my trusted sister, Rosa and whisked off one of the babies. I felt that I was helping Paula too, for she had confided to me her problems. Of course she had not told me about the father but she did utter his name during the delivery. Now, when I heard from my sister that she was informed by Pedro that the Captain was fighting a battle for custody of his child, I knew that I had evidence which would surely prove that the children were his. So that is the reason which made me endure this journey to Portugal with Pedro and Lavina. I know for sure that Paula would have wanted this all along.

Eventually, the verdict was given in Lino's favour. And this verdict was met with much applause from every corner of the Courtroom. In the commotion, Bufon pounced on Paulina and dragged her to the entrance and was making a getaway. Even before the shouts had reached the Brazilian security guard who was guarding the exit from the court, he rushed towards him and brought him down in a flying tackle.

Everything went the way Lino had prayed for. Even Amorous would no longer be a threat to them. The security guard, Rui, was actually a former jail warden in Brazil. In fact he had lost his job, when there was a jail break during his shift. And the persons who had escaped were Bufon and an African slave wanted for murder.

Rui had personally searched for Bufon, but had lost his trail in Macau. Rui had also learnt that he was into occult. Now after so many years, he had at last arrested the man who had escaped, perhaps due to his negligence.

Helena's family had taken good care of Paula's house and Lino spent a month there. By now, both Paulina and Lavina had accepted him as their father. Although Paulina was treated very well by Amarella, it did not take her too long to bond with her lost sister Lavina. The bonding between them made it a lot easier to separate from Amarella.

Meanwhile, Adeline took the captain's option of being the children's' governess. After visiting some of her relatives in Portugal, she too joined them on their journey back to Goa.

The journey back home was very satisfying. Father and daughters had lots to talk about. Lino told little Paulina and Lavina all about their dear mother. Most of their evenings on board the ship were spent sitting on the deck beneath the gigantic sails, telling stories.

Paulina was very excited at the prospect of going back to Goa "Papa, why did Mama leave us?" she asked sadly.

"If she hears that I have been found, will she come back to us?"

"My dear *burbuletta*, your Mama is now one of those stars up there in the heavens. Can you see that large twinkling star . . . that must be her now, smiling at us. When we leave this world, we too will change into stars, and be reunited with your mother once again".

The response made both Paulina and Lavina very happy and they waved out to the star gleefully.

EPILOGUE:

So strong was the love of the villagers of Oddavel for Paula that they decided to immortalize her name by changing the name of their village to Dona Paula. Even the Portuguese government accepted to formally uphold the villagers' petition.

The old dock at Dona Paula was festooned with colourful streamers of crepe paper. At the end of the dock, against the backdrop of the cliff from where Paula had been pushed to her death, was placed a bamboo arch bedecked with roses and ferns. Beneath the arch stood a priest, with a bible in his hand, waiting for the bridal couple to arrive. A little beyond the arch stood an old shrine dedicated to the holy cross, with its niche filled with candles and the cross almost invisible under a mass of marigolds.

In front of the priest were placed two chairs decorated with white satin bows. A few feet away, were a few rows of chairs occupied by family and close friends of the couple. A few whispers could be heard as the older ladies exchanged gossip.

Suddenly there was a blast from the buglers from the army band, announcing the arrival of the bride and groom on the scene. A beautifully decorated horse drawn carriage pulled up behind the assembly followed closely by another. Everyone assembled there were immediately taken up by the Abranches twins who were the flower girls dressed in red organza, with floral crowns as hair bands. Their golden locks of hair bounced merrily as they went about their duty of casting rose petals in front of the bridal couple.

Lieutenant Mariano appeared absolutely peaceful inspite of his handicap and limped cheerfully alongside his lovely bride Linda. The glowing Linda dressed in satin and lace looked angelic as she floated down the aisle on Mariano's arm. Following close behind him was Lino and Clara. The sadness in their eyes was unmistakable but they were all smiles for their friends' sake.

Lino looked at the twins lovingly as they giggled and teased each other, throwing rose petals at each other instead of the floor in front of the bridal couple. The two were being thoroughly spoilt by all the attention that they were receiving from Pedro, Ana and the rest of the Abranches household. Everyone in the village adored them. The twins reminded them of their sweet mother Paula.

Lino looked at the sad but elegant Clara. For the first time since her rescue from Madagascar, she was returning his smiles. She had grown very fond of the twins and the three seemed to get along fine with each other. He himself was attracted to her in a strange way, although he brushed aside the thoughts, replacing them with Paula's. As he gazed at the top of the cliff, thinking of that fateful day when his life collapsed around him, the gentle breeze seemed to whisper a message from Paula, "I will always be with you but the girls need a mother. Please carry on with your life".

His thoughts were disturbed by a little tug at his hands as Clara reminded him that they still had a few more steps to go before they could reach the altar . . .

There was much dancing and drinking after the nuptials. Lino and the girls made a quiet exit from the wedding party to bid the sun adieu before another sleepless night would engulf him. As usual, the sunset was spectacular from the cliff. Paulina and Lavina were delighted with the whole phenomenon and clapped gleefully as the huge ball of orange sank slowly beneath the horizon. Lino was too engrossed in his thoughts and for a moment did not realize that Clara was standing right behind him. For a moment he froze, as the soft light of dusk reflected on her satin dress made her appear to float. It was as if Paula had decided his future for him. As the girls clapped in glee, Lino and Clara embraced each other passionately.

It was as if morning had already broken!

BIBLIOGRAPHY

Goa Cultural Patterns—Marg Publications (1983)

A India Portugueza Vol. 1 and 2—A. Lopes Mendes

Beyond The Self; *Santa Casa De Misericordia De Goa*-Fatima Da Silva Gracias

An Historical and Archaeological Sketch of the City of Goa-Jose Nicolau De Fonseca

Farar Far; Local Resistance to the Colonial Hegemony in Goa 1510 - 1912—Pratima Kamat

Goa and Portugal; their cultural Links—Edited by Charles J. Borges, Helmut Feldmann

Note: Various authors' articles, on the Internet have also influenced the author. Mentioning all the links here would be a huge task however, the author is very thankful for the immense research and study conducted by scholars and historians on Goa that is now freely available for reference on the web.

Special thanks to Dr. Teotonio R. D'Souza of Xavier Cultural Research Centre (Porvorim-Goa) who had helped with the research for my Bachelor Of Architecture final year thesis 'A MUSEUM FOR GOAN RELIGIOUS ARTS AND CRAFTS', which proved helpful even for this book.

Glossary

Adambo (Konkani) - The security crossbar behind doors

Admiràvel - Admirable

Asante *(Swahili)* - Thank you

Auto Da Fé - Solemn act of faith

Avenida Dom João Castro - John Castro Avenue

Avózinha - grandmother

Bom Viagem - Good journey

Bom dia - Good morning

Broa de Milho - Bread of maize

Burbuletta - butterfly

Caldo - soup

Campo Santo Lazaro - St. Lazaro's field

Capitão - Captain

Capitão do Porto - Captain of ports

Carreira de India - Sea-route to India

Casa de Misericordia de Goa - The Holy House of Mercy

Cidade de Goa - City of Goa

Cravate - A tie

Casçado - Portuguese married to a native Indian

Castelo Santo Jorge - Castle of St George

Disgraça! - Disgrace!

Donzelas - damsel; virgin

Então! - Well then!

Escrivão - Clerk (esp. in the court)

Eu sou - I am

Familiares do Santo Officio - Fellow of the Holy Office

Feiticeiro - sorcerer

Fidalgo - Nobleman

Firangi *(Konkani)* - Foreigner

Ghumot *(konkani)* - pot shaped earthern drum

Grande - Big

Ilha de Moçambique - Island of Mozambique

Joie-de-vivre - Joy of life

Kanji *(Konkani)* - rice broth

Kshatriyas *(Hindi)* - Warrior class (Hindu Caste system)

Mãe - Mother

Maki - A lemur in Malagasy

Merde - shit

Meu Amor - My Love

Meus amigos - My friends

Meus Deus! - My God!

Monsignor - Title of honour conferred on some prelates

Morgado - Beloved

Nau - Large sail ship

Obrigado - Thank you

Oddlem Ghor *(konkani)* - Big House

Orfaas del Rei - Orphans of the king

Olá Senhora - Hello madame

Padre - Priest

Padrinho - godfather

Palaçio - Palace

Pardãos - Old Portuguese currency

Pombeiros - Dealers

Porteira - Doorkeeper

Praça de Leitão - Pig square

Provedor - Superintendent of a charitable institution

Puta - Whore

Quartel - *(Police)* station

Quanta custa - How much does this cost?

Recolhimento do Nossa Senhora de Serra - Retirement home of our Lady of the mountain.

Regente - Governor

Reis Magos - The three kings

Rua Direita - Main Street

Senado - Municipal Council

Senhor - Sir

Tão bella! - How good!

Tia - Aunt

Tinto - Market place

Tio - Uncle

Todop baz - female traditional dress